Magnus Jones

MAGNUS JONES

Alain Wolf

RESOURCE *Publications* • Eugene, Oregon

MAGNUS JONES

Resource Publications
An Imprint of Wipf and Stock Publishers
199 W. 8th Ave., Suite 3
Eugene, OR 97401

www.wipfandstock.com

PAPERBACK ISBN: 979-8-3852-7096-5
HARDCOVER ISBN: 979-8-3852-7097-2
EBOOK ISBN: 979-8-3852-7098-9

VERSION NUMBER 042926

CHAPTER I

The Paine Anglia University or "PAU" is madly fond of its acronyms. They are so frequently used in the speech of faculty and students alike that a visitor, on first entering campus, must be inducted into their meaning by being shown a glossary entitled "The Acronyms of Paine Anglia University, Home of the Incredible." Some of these are easy enough to understand. "EDU," for example, stands for the "Department of Education." Others do not trip off the tongue so easily; the "English Literature Department" is known as "ELDWC" (English, Literature, Drama, and Writing Creatively), and the "Department of Linguistics" as "CSTIC" (Communication Studies, Translation, and Intercultural Communication).

"Lecturer in Communication Studies!" said Dr. Magnus Jones at a staff meeting one day. "How did you come up with that one?"

"The students were put off by the word 'linguistics,'" said Professor Lehideux, "and if you must know, it had an effect on recruitment."

"But linguistics is what I teach," said Dr. Jones, "and 'communication studies' most definitely is not."

"Be that as it may," said Lehideux, "our Head of School and the executive team have come to the decision that a new name was required for the Department of Linguistics. From now on, it will be known as the Department of Communication Studies, Translation, and Intercultural Communication or CSTIC."

They were seated at opposite ends of a large seminar table, at the top of which sat the triumvirate by which the department was effectively run, the head of school, Dr. Michael Sedley, whose indolence was only exceeded by a gluttonous appetite, Professor André Lehideux, the unprepossessing French lecturer, and Dr. Adam Grieve, who was known to be a genius in his field, though he never completed the articles he wrote, let alone got them into print. The seminar room was small and stuffy. An assortment of lecturers had ventured opposition, mainly to do with the pronunciation of "CSTIC" which, they said, was either too long if each letter was pronounced individually, or would inevitably be pronounced "stick" by students. Dr. Coffey, the plucky Northern Irish tutor, said that "CSTIC" reminded him, for some reason he was unable to account for, of cystitis, which only resulted in Professor Lehideux ignoring his comment and turning his back on the offending speaker. Professor Daphne Ifantidou, sitting next to Dr. Coffey, also thought the new acronym reminded her of a medical condition and was still laughing when she expressed her support for Dr. Jones. Daphne had acquired an international reputation for her academic work on how to motivate students to learn foreign languages and could always be relied upon to rally round her favourite Magnus. They both had Cambridge PhDs and usually came to similar conclusions as far as the running of the department was concerned, much to the dismay of the "executive team."

"But with respect," she said, which usually indicated she was about to show a total lack of it, "this is an erasure of our research interests in the department and Dr. Jones is quite right that 'communication studies' has very little to do with what we as research staff currently offer."

Ms. Sheena Taylor, a large, blonde Australian woman in very tight jeans and an intimate relationship with the greasy pole, was naturally in favour of the change of name. She may not have her PhD, yet, but she taught a number of courses on communication across languages and the new name better reflected what was *actually* taught in the department. This was, of course, intended as a dig at the lecturers who had PhDs and did not do as much teaching as she did.

"We are not talking about quantity of teaching here," interrupted Professor Ifantidou archly, "but about how it needs to be inspired by our research interests."

Ms. Taylor knew when to capitulate, but not before remarking that after all, South Anglia University ("SAU," pronounced "sow") had just been renamed as Paine Anglia University ("PAU," pronounced "Pow!"), in the same way, without consultation. In this, she was right. South Anglia University with its acronym "SAU" had been the constant butt of jokes among students on account of its agricultural connotations, and the university had been given a new name by the recently appointed vice-chancellor, Professor Charles Ramsbottom. The professor had hoped that the new Paine Anglia University with its powerful acronym "PAU" would . . . well . . . energise the university. Indeed, the old SAU had been perceived as affecting student recruitment.

"The old SAU had been perceived as affecting student recruitment," said Dr. Jones, imitating, "For the love of God, do we really think that 'PAU' is better than 'SAU' and that it makes the slightest bit of difference as to whether a prospective applicant will choose us over another university?'

This was met with dead silence. Professor Lehideux gave a sideway glance at Dr. Sedley and there was a tacit understanding that they would have to show this meddlesome upstart who was boss. About Professor Ifantidou nothing much could be done. Only students' complaints about her reputedly flamboyant teaching methods would get rid of her. In a previous meeting, Dr. Grieve was adamant that one single hour of her teaching must defy all the principles of the university's diversity training programme, but he could not prove anything, and would have to wait until a student lodged a complaint against her. They all agreed that this was the best way to go about it with Dr. Sedley concluding that Professor Ifantidou would in the end be worn down by attrition. He nodded repeatedly, obviously satisfied with his mode of expression. This was remarkable exertion on his part, and soon after he was seen to fall back into his usual state of somnolence. The other members of the triumvirate did not mind this in the slightest, and the departmental gossip, without Dr. Sedley's contributions, continued apace.

At the end of the fruitless staff meeting, Dr. Magnus Jones had walked back to his office through campus, looking in wonder at the beauty of the foliage made even more beautiful by the comparative ugliness of the concrete around him. The buildings of PAU, 1960s in design, were listed and would be preserved forever. They had fallen into disrepair, soon after being built, at great cost to the university. Dr. Jones's sense of aesthetics had been honed in Cambridge as that which is uplifting and religious. There was nothing religious at PAU and, he reflected, nothing uplifting, either. As he walked, he invested the concrete with the glowing honey-coloured stone of his former college. Nostalgia. Dr. Jones was not particularly given to such feelings. He had managed to avoid nostalgia in his recent research on film adaptations of Jane Austen. He had also managed to avoid the pitfalls of some of the latest trends in research. Jane Austen's work made more palatable to the contemporary readership by means of musings on the provenance of sugar seemed particularly misguided. He had read too many books the titles of which started with "Jane Austen and . . ." whatever else the author was interested in. So no nostalgia, no ideology. Just language. But Cambridge often slipped through his consciousness. In the early days of his appointment at PAU, he had sent an email to Professor Lehideux in which he had inadvertently referred to the "spring semester" as the "Easter term." Lehideux had written back reminding him that PAU was a secular institution and that religious terminology like "Easter" had best be avoided in the public sphere.

"This is not France," replied Dr. Jones, "and in this country at least the Church is part of the state."

"Sometimes, I don't understand how somebody with your level of education can be religious," said Lehideux, popping his angular head through Dr. Jones's office door.

"Sometimes, I don't understand how someone who teaches communication across languages and cultures is so closed to religious cultures," retorted Dr. Jones.

"I do not know how you dare to speak to me like zis," said Lehideux, his French accent getting the better of him.

"I am only saying that it is inexcusable that someone who claims to be open to other cultures fails at the first hurdle of dialogue between secular and religious cultures."

The discussion had ended with shouts of "outrageous" on the part of Lehideux and with Dr. Jones keeping icily coherent. An enraged Lehideux reported the *micro-aggression* to Dr. Sedley. Something had to be done to rein in Dr. Jones. He would never have been appointed if his religious fanaticism had been known. Considering he was still a probationer, there should be as much opposition as possible to him being made a permanent lecturer. Dr. Sedley, slowly rousing himself out of the torpor caused by eating a considerable sausage roll accompanied by a most succulent Cornish pasty, the crumbs of which were still in evidence on his shirt, expressed his full agreement with the professor. His indolence, however, did not extend to anything more determinate than the repeated exclamation: "Oh, I do agree!"

"And we must scrutinise him for any administrative misdemeanour," cried Lehideux exasperated.

"Oh, I do agree!" said Dr. Sedley one more time.

Dr. Sedley was so odd a mixture of abstract benevolence and practical wickedness that the experience of ten years as a lecturer had been insufficient to teach him anything worthwhile about integrity, academic or otherwise. He was content to let himself be ruled by the ambitions of others as they accorded with his own. The business of his life was to climb up the career ladder of the university; its solace was eating and drinking.

CHAPTER II

It was a fine, clear spring evening. Magnus Jones pulled the door of his office shut towards him, but then opened it again and went back in. He had left the student admission forms on the supervision table in the middle of the room, and decided it would be safer to lock them in his filing cabinet.

The previous head of school, Dr. Anderson, a benevolent, if an evangelical Christian, had given Magnus the role of postgraduate admissions tutor.

"You're a new man," he said, "stepping in dead men's shoes, but the right man for this. I mean, you've even interviewed applicants for Cambridge University, so this should be a piece of cake."

He had explained that the role involved reading through the personal statements and forms of students who had applied to do an MA in Linguistics at PAU—this was before the MA in Communication Studies, Translation, and Intercultural Communication—and deciding whether their applications were successful or not. When the time came for Magnus to take on his role, Ben Anderson sadly and somewhat abruptly died.

"This is most irregular, a mere probationer in such a position of authority," said Dr. Sedley resentfully, "but since it has all been agreed before Dr. Anderson's departure, I will not go against the decision."

During his first few weeks in the post, Magnus had relished his new responsibilities immensely. He was careful to exercise his judgement wisely, rejecting those applicants who showed signs of weakness in expressing themselves, or did not show much interest in the field of linguistics. His typical comment was: "The student has not demonstrated sufficient interest and aptitude in the proposed course of study." But the role of admissions tutor soon turned out to be a poisoned chalice. It all started when one of his filled-in admission forms was returned to him by the administrator of the "Postgraduate Embedded Team" ("PET"). Magnus had not quite worked out what "PET" was, or what purpose it served. He had been told the team worked alongside academics to provide them with the support they needed. From what he had experienced so far, the "embedded team" seemed either embedded in inactivity, or unnecessarily interfering.

A note was attached to the returned form: "Please reconsider your decision to reject this student. She has attained all the required grades in her undergraduate Chinese university degree, she has excellent references from her previous tutors, and has passed the English language examination for international students." Magnus's reply had been immediate and, as we know, immediacy of response leads without fail to hot words. It read: "I have not so far come across one Chinese student's application which does not contain outstanding grades, and tutors' references so glowing that one would think the entire Chinese student population consists of future Nobel Prize winners. My rejection is based on the only thing that discriminates between the applicants, and that is the quality of their personal statement and its phraseology. Wherever the statements display weaknesses in language or argument, I feel justified in rejecting the applicant." There was no response. A few days later, Magnus was summoned to Dr. Sedley's office.

"It would appear," Dr. Sedley began in an affectedly benign tone, "that you are turning down international applicants on the basis of their proficiency in English."

"Not just that," said Magnus, "as you will see from my comments I turn them down on their inability to express their argument coherently and, well . . ."

"Are you aware," Dr. Sedley interrupted more angrily, "that under no circumstances are you to assess international students on the basis of their language skills if they have fulfilled the criteria required by this university, that is passing the 'International English Language' examination?"

"Then these criteria are not sufficient for them to engage with the rigorous demands of study at MA level at a university in the UK. Not a year goes by without me or my colleagues having to fail such students in considerable numbers. This is what I am trying to stop happening."

"May I suggest that you are missing the point, Magnus? When these students come to us, they are required to go on a three weeks' intensive course in 'English for Academic Purposes' which enables them to cope thereafter with the demands of their proposed course of study."

Magnus made no answer. Dr. Sedley was forced to conclude that international postgraduate students could only be rejected on the basis of poor grades in their undergraduate degree and a demonstrably clear lack of aptitude in the proposed field of study.

"By 'lack of aptitude,' I mean that the applicant does not make any reference whatsoever to the said field of study, or mistakenly proposes to study in a subject we do not offer. This is the remit of your role."

Dr. Jones remained silent.

"Is this all you have to say?" asked Dr. Sedley.

"I have nothing further to say," replied Magnus.

"No, indeed," said Dr. Sedley, "but if you continue to reject applicants at the rate of knots, I will have to ask you to resign from your post as MA Admissions Tutor. In the meantime, the PET administrator will send me your rejections if she feels that they are unjustified and do not align with our criteria. I hope that this clarifies matters."

Magnus could see pearls of perspiration forming on Dr. Sedley's balding forehead.

"It certainly makes the university's position clear," said Dr. Jones. "It makes my conscience less so."

"Damn your conscience, man!" said Dr. Sedley in exasperation. "These students pay your salary, for God's sake; this is all that can be said for your conscience. I am seriously disappointed with your attitude."

Before Dr. Sedley had finished speaking, Magnus Jones rose with an inward smile that illuminated his face though he was not smiling. This was not lost on Dr. Sedley who only managed a sigh in the knowledge that problems lay ahead and that this issue had not been satisfactorily resolved.

And so it was better after all that the admission forms were locked safely in his filing cabinet. They contained the usual amount of rejections and were ready to be sent to PET. Just as Magnus was about to leave, there was a knock at the door. Daphne sauntered in before he could say anything. She was like one of those Cambridge thesps he used to hang out with, each new meeting starting with a hug and punctuated with an airy kiss and a "how are you, darling?"

"Not that good actually," said Magnus, endeavouring to recover himself. "It's Sedley; he's threatening to make me resign as admissions tutor because I reject too many international students."

"Well, how apposite! As it happens, I've found something out which ought to provide you with some ammunition at least," she said in the conspiratorial tone that presaged breaking news. "Do you remember that Chinese student who failed all of her MA modules last year?"

"You mean the student I rejected and who for some reason still managed to get a place on our MA programme?"

"Yes, and you said that some Chinese students are like boomerangs: no matter how much you reject them, they still manage to turn up on our courses."

"Bit of a mystery how they keep turning up here despite being rejected."

"I think I may be about to unravel it. You see, I have interviewed some Chinese students for my research on language motivation, and my findings about what the university has been up to will quite bowl you over, if that's the expression you use in English."

"So what is it, Daphne?"

"You'll find out all in good time when the research is completed, not before then. Now don't start buggering me, please."

"Don't you mean 'bugging me'?"

"Sorry, darling, I always get the two mixed up, though not in practice, of course."

Daphne Ifantidou was impulsively lovely, her mistakes infectious, and one laughed with her rather than at her. They parted, agreeing that Magnus would have to wait until Daphne felt it was an appropriate time to disclose her findings.

"It won't be long," she said, "before the mystery of the boomerang Chinese students is finally solved."

Magnus's mind was now relieved from the heavy weight that had followed his encounter with Dr. Sedley, and after half an hour's quiet reflection by the side of the campus lake, a sense of satisfaction filled him which was mainly to do with the feeling of work well done. When they designed the campus of Paine Anglia, the architects had at least got one thing right. The halls of residence connected by walkways were built on the lakeside. Terraces and cafes looked out on the banks, and students could often be seen reading there at the water's edge where willow herb, meadowsweet, and bulrushes grew in abundance. There were Canada geese begging for food and other birds which delighted Magnus. The halls were referred to as colleges and had all been named after famous Norfolk men and women, or local places of interest: Julian College was the first to be built and consequently had the more spacious student accommodation. Holkham College came next, then Cavell College, named after the Anglican nurse turned martyr, and lastly Blakeney College, the rooms of which were considerably smaller as funds had dwindled when it was built. At the northern end of the lake stood Paine Central Hall which, illuminated at night, looked like a flying saucer.

Now, as he emerged from the network of interconnected walkways, Magnus was able to consider driving all the way back to his North Norfolk home in East Holton. Gwendolen, the old lavender blue Commer camper van, was very visible in the university car park. He looked at it with affectionate admiration. He had managed to keep her ever since his student days and it had almost broken his heart to erase some of the drawings his friends had painted over it, a bee, a huge daisy, a go-kart when he had her repainted. Still, Gwendolen looked better than ever and was ready for another trip abroad during the Easter vac. Magnus, after the misery of the afternoon, found himself at the wheel of his beloved vehicle and on his way to Holton Hall.

CHAPTER III

Magnus drove along bathing in a pensive mood. The warmth of the evening light permeated through Gwendolen the camper van and he felt relaxed and hopeful. The warm weather of spring was likely to last into summer. He breathed in the freedom of the wide open fields around him. Gwendolen pootled along slowly, and the muntjac deer did not risk their lives quite so much crossing the road. The clear air was intoxicating. As he drove deeper and deeper into the Norfolk countryside, it was as if he had sloughed off his urban self, crossing into another world of undulating fields, flat enough to foreground the numerous towered churches on small promontories. The churches dotted the horizon as far as the eye could see. He often counted them, one church, Farningham, two churches, Thurgarton, three churches, Erpingham. He turned off the main road to drive through Harvington. The street dipped to a barely noticeable ford, a world of moss and ivy which filled him with a sense of that which is beyond. Gwendolen made a splashing sound in the water and Magnus felt the closeness to those whom he had loved and had recently gone before him. It was as if only a thin veil separated him from them. Their words of comfort, formlessly articulated in his mind, made him unafraid of his own death. The drive took him through the last hamlet of Erpingham past the community shop open since the early eighteenth century; two centuries of uninterrupted shopping, tea-drinking, and cake-eating. Jane Austen could have stopped there, he thought, and drunk sugared tea in her cotton dresses.

When he arrived at Holton Hall rectory, Alessandro, the Sicilian estate manager, was waiting for him, pruning roses in the front garden.

"There you are," he said. "Thought you'd never get here."

"Tedious meeting this afternoon," said Magnus, thinking Alessandro was speaking to him more and more as if they were man and wife these days. "Are you coming to Mattins on Sunday? Rev. Leigh's curate is conducting the service."

"Is he now?" Alessandro's smirk indicated he had no wish to attend.

"Thought I'd warn you anyhow. Come on, let's have some tea or maybe something stronger. I am starving."

"I have made red pasta and got us a bottle of wine to go with it."

"Perfect. Just what the doctor ordered."

Magnus and Alessandro had shared a flat for the last two years of their degree at Cambridge and then for another two years as they were completing their postgraduate studies. In those four years of sharing in the difficulties and the joys of getting degrees and enjoying university life, never a cross word had passed between them. Alessandro had just left his native Sicily and saw his new life in Cambridge as if it were a honeymoon. He was tallish and his dark blond hair lightened in the summer. His skin, already fair, turned a golden brown. When people remarked that he did not look Sicilian at all, he'd say the Normans had invaded the country and he was descended from them. Magnus next to him looked quite the dark man of Gothic novels, cast in the Hebraic mould, Alessandro, the Hellenic.

Alessandro had been attracted to Magnus ever since he'd set eyes on him in the junior common room, but they had never spoken of it. What developed instead was an unshakeable and spiritual friendship of which Lady Agatha, Magnus's mother, was a little suspicious.

"It is perfectly fine for Alessandro to be the estate manager here," she said. "Far be it from me to pry into your private affairs, but I would like grandchildren and since the usual way of getting them is with a woman, it would be good if you started the conventional procedures towards getting a wife. Sharing your life with another man is not one of them."

Magnus agreed. Henrietta, the woman his mother suggested for him, was a suitable candidate for marriage after all and would do very well. There had been signs that she liked him, too. Marriage had not hitherto been a priority. As a second son, he'd had his work cut out for him, having to qualify for an occupation which suited him and this had not left much time for courting. But this was certainly the time to make his advances known to her.

Henrietta had now worked for the family firm, Elliott and Jones, for over a year, and, most desirably, was distantly related to royalty. Although Lady Agatha did not explicitly say so, such an alliance would signal the family's return to the aristocratic connections she herself had so blithely disdained in a rush of youthful love and 1960s egalitarianism, both of which *démangeaisons* she had now quite got over. It must be said, Lady Agatha Jones had made what had been considered at the time an imprudent match. Daughter of Sir Harvie Elliott, baronet, she had been known in the village of Holton as Miss Agatha Elliott, and when, on her father's death, she inherited Holton Hall, she decided to marry a Mr. Edmund Jones, the owner of Jones & Lewis, the most successful department store in the nearby market town of Holton. Some had thought this was an unfortunate misalliance, but the marriage had been a happy one. Mr. Edmund Jones developed the shop into a business, now called Elliott and Jones, which offered absolutely everything from a brewery to beauty and building products. On account of his services to trade and industry, he had been knighted Sir Edmund Jones, and Mrs. Agatha Jones regained her credentials as Lady Agatha Jones. This unexpected return into the gentry marked in her a *prise de conscience*. As she aged, she resolved not to become an imperious Lady Bracknell, tempting as this may be. The permissive society had made her tolerant of most diverse ways of living, fond of the occasional liqueur and intense partying. She, nonetheless, held on to the basic Christian principles of love of neighbour and the sovereignty of nations, the violation of which did indeed seem like the worst excesses of the French Revolution.

The next day passed in the quietness of the rectory, reading, gardening, and cooking. Alessandro visited from the tenanted cottage next door, and so did Magnus's elder brother, Aled, who lived in the great house with his wife, Isabella, and two lovely, sporty, enthusiastic boys, Tristan and Owain. Magnus admired Aled and Isabella. With the help of Alessandro, they managed the estate, looked after the tenants' cottages and the nearby dairy farm. Holton Hall was a going concern but more than that. It was the centre of activities in the village. Alongside the vicar, Rev. Leigh, fêtes were organised and Ceilidhs were danced in the old hall. The survival of village life depended on the family, and Aled, the future owner of Holton Hall, though not a squire, was called upon to act as one.

"You coming to the service tomorrow?" asked Aled, striding through the rectory garden in his muddy boots.

"Wouldn't miss it for anything," said Magnus.

"Thought I'd warn you the curate is conducting the service, and from what I have seen, we could be in for an interesting sermon."

"I know; Alessandro is not coming."

"How am I not surprised? See you tomorrow, then."

The next morning, a fine Mother's Day crisp-and-clear kind of morning, took Magnus and Alessandro, who had after all decided to come along, on the walk from the rectory to the Church of St. Nicholas in the grounds of Holton Hall. The rectory was part of Holton Village, but one could access the hall through a little gate at the back used for centuries by the incumbent who officiated in St. Nicholas. The path meandered through meadows and parkland landscaped by Repton and rose gently up to the great house, a small and rare example of a Jacobean manor house. From a distance, one could see the mullioned windows of the manor. As they reached the house, Lady Agatha was already waiting for them on the gravelled drive. At eighty-two years of age, she still looked resplendent. She stood leaning against the pillar of the porch at the entrance of the hall, her hands in the pockets of a pearl-white cardigan loosely hanging over a red and grey tartan skirt. Her shiny white hair made her look translucent in the strong morning light.

"I thought you weren't coming," she said, addressing herself to Alessandro.

"It is Mother's Day and this prevails over anything else," said Alessandro who longed to be at home celebrating it with his mother.

"Too right, too right, and so it should," said Lady Agatha. Her affection for Alessandro had grown over the years, though she continued to perceive him as the main obstacle to her son's future happiness with a wife and children.

They all three proceeded across the bridge to the north of Holton Hall where a stream formed a kind of natural ha-ha to stop the cows grazing in the park. A few hundred yards further north stood the Church of St. Nicholas with its ruined tower and surviving chancel. This was the church where Magnus had worshipped all his life and seeing it emerging above the rolling landscape was a joy in itself, another place where the dividing line between the this-wordly and the transcendent became tenuous. The interior had been unaltered for the last two centuries, walls were painted a luminous Georgian green, and plain wooden pews on each side of the narrow nave led to the communion table. There was something of a *via media* Anglicanism about it, shunning the excesses of Rome without sinking into the deprivations of low-church Protestantism. Today, the church was decorated with bunches of daffodils which would be distributed to the women in the congregation at the end of the service.

The curate, Rev. Andrew Bold, met them at the entrance. He was a sleek young man, his hair gathered up in a bun at the top of his head. He came from North London and had been trained as a vicar in a liberal-minded theological college in Cambridge. He had led services in the benefice before, but not yet preached here, and this was to be his first sermon. Rev. Leigh, the incumbent vicar, was also greeting members of the congregation, and was confident that all would go well though, being a trusting kind of fellow, he had not read the sermon himself.

The service began well enough but then the sermon was peppered with references to the fashionable ideas of the Church of England hierarchy. Andrew Bold was very fond of words ending in "ism." In an emotional peroration, he invited the parishioners to reflect on how they may be perpetrators of racism.

"To what extent," he asked, "were they responsible for the injustices of the world two hundred years ago? Wasn't our Lord and Saviour a model of inclusivism himself?" he cried.

Lady Agatha had a bunch of keys which she kept about her tartan skirt. She gave them a sudden jerk, and they jangled most sonorously. Every time a word with an "ism" came up in the sermon, the jangling was heard.

At the end of the service, Andrew Bold, who also had an aversion to the language of the King James Bible, blessed the congregation replacing the words "passeth all understanding" by saying:

"The peace of God, which *is beyond* all understanding, keep your hearts and minds in the knowledge and love of God and of his Son Jesus Christ our Lord."

The keys were given another merciless jerk, and the service was thankfully over. During the little gathering over coffee, Lady Agatha approached the curate.

"Vicar," she said, "you gave me quite a turn with your isms."

"Oh, so you had difficulties with my sermon, Lady Agatha."

"I had no *difficulties* whatsoever, but we do have a gospel to proclaim. Jesus didn't need 'isms' to save a woman from being stoned to death."

Fortunately, it was time to be gone. Lady Agatha was off first, and she could breathe outside for a few minutes. "Insufferable man!" was her immediate observation. "Inclusivism, indeed! A presumptuous upstart with all his airs and graces, his ludicrous hair and fashionable talk. And the blessing was the final straw. The peace of God which is beyond all understanding! Have you heard anything like it? No understanding of English, no understanding of nuances. Worse than I had supposed."

All this ran disconnectedly through her thoughts and by the time Magnus had caught up with her, she was tolerably able to speak to him coherently.

"Well, my dear," she began, "I thought the service was very badly done."

"I dare say he has a great deal to learn, Mama. But he has been living in Islington and is infected with the ideas of a particular set. Of course, I come across them regularly at PAU and am much more used to his offences than you are."

"And his offences will occupy my mind for the time to come" was all that Lady Agatha could manage before Alessandro joined them holding a bunch of daffodils Reverend Bold had given to him.

"Well, you *have* been favoured," said Lady Agatha, and Alessandro, understanding the full extent of her meaning, winced.

"He seems a very foolish sort of man," he said.

This was one occasion when Lady Agatha's opinion of Alessandro grew more favourably towards him than he could possibly have known.

CHAPTER IV

When Magnus awoke the following morning, he found, as consciousness slowly returned, that he was full of optimism. It was as if the night had brought good tidings all around. Putting on the armour of light, he had a vigorous shower, slipped on his best corduroy trousers, a crisp white shirt and his favourite royal blue jacket. Then he looked out on another damp morning. Gwendolen-the-campervan was averse to wet weather and would not start easily. And so it was in a spluttering kind of way that Magnus left Holton. As he reached the city and drove along past the surly rows of suburban houses, his thoughts turned to Daphne Ifantidou. He had received an email over the weekend in which she said she had finally received written confirmation that her article was accepted for publication and was now at liberty to reveal what she'd found out about Paine Anglia University (she never used the acronym, "PAU") during the course of her research. Recalling what had happened in his office, it seemed to Magnus that it was Daphne who had imparted to him his newly found sense of confidence. He did not quite know why. Her eccentricities were liberating, disclosing an alternative possibility of being. This was good for the soul.

He reached PAU still in that general state of felicity and good will to all. Even the sight of little Dr. Coffey in his cycling shorts was not altogether unpleasant. James Coffey used the shower in the basement every morning and emerged fresh-faced, tousled and muscular in the corridors of PAU. His energy dissolved the general sloth of the morning and Magnus as a rule enjoyed his company. It was invigorating and made one want to emulate him.

Magnus parked Gwendolen on a grassy verge near some bushes. The university had recently allowed students to use the staff car park. This had led to a lack of parking spaces and members of staff frantically parking their cars wherever they could before class. Altercations followed, and the parking attendant who spent his time fruitfully taking photographs of cars parked in "inappropriate" places had had his phone snatched from him by an irate lecturer from the "English, Drama, and Writing Creatively" department (ELDWC). The lecturer had straightaway gone to the security lodge, thrown the phone down onto the desk, and given whoever happened to be there merry hell in the most colourful of language which, some said, even included Elizabethan swear words. Of course, the "incident," as it was referred to, was entirely caught on camera as a result of which the lecturer was summoned by the human resources department (HR) for a disciplinary meeting. It was later rumoured that Human Resources had acted most inhumanly. The head of HR, Mrs. Miranda Slope, had forced the hapless lecturer to watch the video of himself blustering and gesticulating, and had accused him of aggressive behaviour towards the female security officer. This, Mrs. Slope added officiously, was a legally protected characteristic under the Equality Act. Luckily, the head of ELDWC, Professor Gardiner, was also present. He did not much care for the Equality Act and protected characteristics which made him think of French cheeses. He took pity on the lecturer and, much to Mrs. Slope's disgust, declined to give him a formal warning.

So far all that had happened to Magnus was a note on Gwendolen's windscreen advising him that he would be banned from using the car park if he carried on parking his car inappropriately. Since the car park was full this morning, he decided to wing it and park "inappropriately" again. If he got banned, he'd be saving himself some money, the monthly parking fee being considerable. He'd get a bike and maybe, well, maybe, he'd end up as fit and muscular as Dr. Coffey in the bargain, although cycling shorts were quite out of the question.

He reached the corridor leading to his office and went past Dr. Coffey's open door, surprised that he'd already had time for a shower. James Coffey came out smiling. He was smaller than Magnus, wirier and leaner. His hair was jet black, contrasting with his porcelain white skin. His soft face expressed creative vagueness. He was known to play the violin at concert level. He could be impulsive and emotional with occasional flights of caustic humour and Magnus was attracted by the indeterminacy of his youth. James Coffey's mode of existence was unfathomable to him, and he wished they could be friends.

"Hello," said Dr. Coffey, "how goes it this morning?"

"Fine," said Magnus, "apart from the usual problems with parking. I'm thinking of getting a bike actually. I need to get fit."

"How about we cycle in together then?"

"Well, why not? I am not in your league, though," rejoined Magnus, almost regretting having mentioned the bike, so obvious was James's enthusiasm.

Magnus turned round slowly, unsure if it now was all right to walk away, only to catch sight, above James's shoulders, of Ms. Taylor's hunched figure reverently putting up a poster on her office door. The poster said: "This is a safe space." The vice-chancellor, Professor Ramsbottom, had just sent a university-wide email encouraging members of staff to create safe spaces around the university and Sheena, ever mindful of bandwagons, had been very eager to jump on that one. Magnus reflected that the day was getting better and better in its drollery. Sheena's reputation for safety was not unparalleled. An eco-activist, she was known to have glued herself and some of her students to anything that did not move, roads, petrol pumps, you name it, all in protest against the use of fossil fuels.

"Hi, Sheena," said Magnus who had seen an opportunity for the merciless teasing of his colleague, "Professor Ramsbottom will be pleased. I just had a thought though; does it mean that my office is fundamentally unsafe?"

"Oh, no, I should not think so: it's just an awareness-raising thing, I suppose."

"I see," said Magnus looking at James who seemed very interested in the direction the exchange was taking, "and when are you next flying to Australia then? I am so envious: I'd love to visit there one day."

"Sometime this summer," Sheena said sheepishly, clearly uneasy in the knowledge that flying across the world did not sit easily with her eco-warrior credentials. "Oh, but I do plant trees to offset my carbon emissions."

"And where do you plant them?"

"Well, I don't actually plant them myself; I pay the airline to do so."

"I'd be very interested in finding out more about this tree-planting lark. I suppose it matters where they are planted. We do need fields for food production after all."

"Of course, we do," was all that Sheena could manage before the authoritative sound of clicking shoes interrupted the exchange. It was Daphne, wearing a trouser suit and prodigiously high heels. Her legs thus majestically extended swam into their vision, and Dr. Coffey blushed, seemingly registering a sensual awakening.

"Hi Sheena, darling," said Daphne towering above her, "I saw you yesterday on the BBC. How you managed to glue yourself to that microphone I don't know, but I am relieved to see you've come out of it unscathed.

"Let's go into your office," she added, throwing an affectionate arm round Magnus's shoulders. Sheena muttered something inaudible and quickly retreated into her office, but not before Daphne could get a glimpse of her withered pot plants.

"A very poor example of carbon capture," Daphne was heard guffawing before they entered in the comparatively unsafe space of Magnus's office.

"Dr. Jones," said Daphne, in a tone that exaggerated formality and yet hardly contained her excitement, "the time has come for me to let you in to the secret of the boomerang Chinese students."

Magnus made no answer. Now that the puzzling phenomenon of students turning up on his courses despite not offering them a university place was about to be explained, Magnus felt a paralysing sense of fear.

"Well, don't you want to hear it?" asked Daphne impatiently.

"Of course, I do, but I am beginning to wonder if it would have been better for me to remain in blissful ignorance."

Daphne, for whom this was invitation enough, proceeded to reveal the dealings of the Postgraduate Embedded Team (PET) with the Chinese Higher Education Bureau in minute details. This was all very corrupt and nauseating but every time Magnus thought he'd heard enough, Daphne came up with some more gruesome revelations. Finally, he begged her to stop. He had heard enough and now must act accordingly. But how? What could he do with these scandalous reports? They were obviously true, or at least could be verified. But what could he do except disclose them at the highest level in his yearly postgraduate admissions report?

"This is precisely what you must do, darling," said Daphne, "this will seal your reputation, you know."

"As a troublemaker who will never get his permanent post, you mean."

"Quite the opposite. You will get through your probationary review. They'll be far too scared of you to touch you, by then. Look, a lot of people admire you for your integrity. I know you will not disappoint."

At that moment, there was a knock at the door and Lifeng Zhu popped his head in.

"Sorry, I see you're busy. I'll come back later," he said.

"I'll be with you in five minutes, Lifeng."

"Actually, what I have to say concerns Daphne as well," said Lifeng as he caught sight of the heels and the legs.

"Then come in and take a seat. What can we do for you? Is it about your application for a PhD?"

"No, I've come here as the bearer of bad news if that's the correct thing to say. Do you remember the Chinese student who failed all of her courses last year?"

"Yes, we were just talking about her. She shouldn't have been here in the first place."

"She's been writing this blog about her experiences at PAU and along with some other Chinese students who also failed your courses, she is spreading the most malicious rumours, advising students against coming to PAU as they will be failed by Dr. Jones, she says, who is anti-Chinese and a racist."

"Is the blog written in Chinese?"

"Yes, which is why I've come to tell you. I've replied to the blog. I said none of it was true, that I was one of your Chinese students and that you'd given me first-class marks for my work, that I was going to do a PhD with you, and that you weren't anti-Chinese. I also said the people spreading rumours just couldn't cope with doing an MA in the UK."

"And did you get a reply?"

"I was told to shut up or else. I'm worried about them. When I said I would not condone these slurs on your reputation, they became really threatening. They're still around. They could make things difficult for me when I get back to China. You could be at risk, too. The Chinese government does sanction foreigners, you know."

"Talk about Sheena creating safe bloody spaces," said Magnus turning to Daphne who gave a start. Magnus rarely swore.

"What's that?" said Lifeng.

"Oh nothing, one of my colleagues is declaring her office to be a 'safe space' on campus, and it all seems pretty meaningless in light of what you've just said."

"I have heard about that. It's a stupid gimmick. They have no idea of what a really unsafe place is. As a gay man and a Christian, I know which country I'd rather be living in."

Magnus looked at Daphne. The moment was too distressing for any more language to make sense of it.

"There, I've said it," said Lifeng finally, a film of tears welling up in his eyes.

Daphne touched his arm lightly.

"Even if I were given the opportunity to stay here after my PhD, I would be worried about the Chinese government's reprisals on my mother. I could not let her endure that."

"I would not have thought this possible," said Magnus ruefully, "I wish we could do something."

Lifeng rose to leave.

"Thank you, Dr. Jones. Look after yourself. You've done what you can. Your lectures have inspired me and I would not be where I am today without you. You've always believed in my work. I could not let anything so blatantly untrue being said about you."

"You look after yourself as well. God bless you, my dear fellow."

"This is truly shocking," said Daphne as soon as the door closed on Lifeng. "All the more reason to put an end to this university's little scam."

Magnus was now firmed up in his resolve to act and speak with determination at the next annual review meeting. It was agreed that he would not send a written copy of the report in advance of the meeting to Dr. Sedley as he was very capable to suppress it and prevent it from being read in its entirety.

The rest of the day was uneventful and Magnus longed to be back in North Norfolk where he could write the report in the comfort of the rectory. As there was no teaching in the afternoon, he decided to leave early and walked back to the car park. The afternoon sun shone fiercely for March. In the distance he could see Gwendolen; she looked as if she'd sunk into the bushes, and he wondered why. As he approached her, he saw the tyres had been slashed, and to his horror, the word "racist" sprayed in black paint across the side door.

When grief subsided, anger took its place. The words of a psalm came to him: "Deliver me from the hand of aliens whose mouth talketh of vain things and their right hand is the hand of falsehood." Then, the first person he thought of was Alessandro. In this moment of despondency, he'd know what to do. Magnus fumbled for his mobile phone and soon the familiar voice answered. He had been right. Alessandro knew just what to do. He'd come to pick him and Gwendolen up with the recovery truck, the one they used for broken-down tractors. It was no problem at all. Magnus should go back to his office, not hang about in the car park. Did he promise to do that? Of course, he'd go back to his office, he'd do just as Alessandro ordered and before he could blurt out further expressions of weepy gratitude, Alessandro was thankfully off the phone.

An hour later, the recovery truck pulled up by Gwendolen with Alessandro looking uncommonly handsome in his old farmer's shirt and muddy boots. In no time at all, they were off in the already fading light of the day.

CHAPTER V

Thanks to Alessandro's ministrations, Gwendolen-the-camp-ervan looked as good as ever. He had managed to get rid of the offending word and as it had slowly dissolved, Magnus's tears ran uncontrollably down his face.

"Come here, you big softie," said Alessandro. They hugged. Magnus, thankful for the morality of practical men doing the little things of this world and making everything well, felt the warmth of his friend and the rough wool of his flannel overshirt. Men of abstractions like him were needed, no doubt, but, as Lady Agatha had said, the woman about to be stoned to death was not saved by isms. One good deed at a time and the injustice of the world melts away. And Magnus kept repeating to himself a curious expression that had come to his mind as he hugged Alessandro: the mustard seed of God's grace, the mustard seed of God's grace.

Two weeks had elapsed during which Magnus had time to mull over exactly how he would present Daphne's revelations to the annual review board meeting.

The meeting was to take place in the registry office boardroom. The CSTIC School began to assemble in the common room which adjoined to the boardroom. Several portraits of ex-vice-chancellors were hung high up and on this sunny afternoon the light fell on their gowns enhancing the PAU colourful academic hoods.

Magnus was in a tweed jacket. He had grown a little fatter round the waist and the jacket had to be left unbuttoned. Still, he thought he looked smart, thoughts of pure vanity which struck him as misplaced considering the gravity of the situation. This was, after all, a daunting experience.

On one side of the room was a sideboard on which stood an urn for hot water and another for coffee. There were biscuits, too.

"Are you having tea or coffee?" asked James Coffey who was standing by his side.

"Coffee, please. I'm going to need something strong."

At that moment Daphne came in causing the general atmosphere to stir. She wore a close-fitting summer dress with a very low *décolleté*. Around her shoulders she wore a kind of white stole which gave her the air of a preacher, a preacher with a low neckline. She surveyed the room with aplomb. Her eyes met with Magnus's. She strode up to him and poured herself what looked like a very strong syrupy espresso from her own flask into a small cup.

Then Sheena Taylor arrived. She had recently been promoted to the posts of senior lecturer and senior pastoral advisor on account of her active participation in Professor Ramsbottom's "safe space" scheme. Dr. Sedley had made all the favourable noises, and it was considered that her enthusiasm far outweighed her lack of academic credentials. This was a meteoric rise which had turned her teeth quite dazzlingly white and her hair much more golden than it used to be. It must be acknowledged that she had been very successful with the "safe spaces." Under her expert guidance, they had mushroomed around campus. Her stated aspiration was that no student should ever be more than two hundred metres from one of them. The Vice-Chancellor, who was pleased she used metres rather than yards, had been supported in this venture by Brickwall, an organisation which advocated the creation of safe spaces in higher education, and which had grown from strength to strength, no one knew how or why. The organisation conferred prestigious and much-sought-after awards on institutions which worked towards fulfilling very specific criteria to be found in the "Brickwall Charter for the Creation of Safe Spaces in Higher Education" (HE). Sheena had led a Brickwall committee, and after spending a few months working tirelessly through the list of criteria with a team of lecturers, she had become the successful recipient of the "PAU! Brickwall Bronze Award."

The CSTIC lecturers were now jostling for drinks by the sideboard. Professor Lehideux pushed through the crowd. He was back from his seminar in French translation, and it had not gone well. He was known to be choleric and impatient with students which made him ill suited to the profession. What's more, he had no awareness of his failings and was inclined to make simple tasks more complex than they needed to be. To the complete bemusement of his students, tests and assignments of all kinds, often unrelated to the main task of translating, proliferated. All this whilst holding on to the firm belief that he was the only one in the school who could lick the students into shape. When things did not go his way, he grew more choleric and as years passed and no one accounted for his behaviour, he had long lost all power of self-control and raised his voice to students in class regularly. Colleagues used the discourse of the day when they referred to him as having an "anger management problem," but nobody saw fit to do anything about it. Today his naturally sallow angular face with deep-set black eyes had grown dark and large areas of purple spread from his neck upwards. This was a sure sign that something had gone wrong. He disappeared into the boardroom without speaking to anybody and muttered something about *liberté*. It must be said that he was an inveterate republican and was so wedded to the idea of "*égalité*" that he wittingly ignored the individual needs of his students and treated them all equally badly.

Finally, Dr. Sedley arrived helping himself to a modest plateful of biscuits. He had brought his own large mug with him which he filled up with coffee to the brim. The school administrator beside him offered to help with his load, but he ignored her. He was the first to enter the boardroom after Professor Lehideux, and was followed by the lecturers of CSTIC with the usual courteous scrimmage at the door.

The boardroom had at its farthest end a little raised area for presenting speakers and there sat the executive team, that is, the team of lecturers with special responsibilities: Dr. Sedley, head of school, Professor Lehideux, research director, Dr. Grieve, director of internationalisation, Ms. Taylor, senior pastoral adviser, and Ms. Christina Huber, dean of employability and German language lecturer. Fräulein Huber was also a rising star who spent most of the day devoting herself to her students' future employment prospects. This left her with very little time to teach her students, as a result of which their knowledge of German declined and left much to be desired. Like Sheena, she had also started writing her PhD thesis, but although this was known to no one at the time, she had developed an ethically problematic way of completing it which involved publishing her best MA students' work.

The first of the presentations was the introduction to the meeting by Dr. Sedley. As he rose to his feet, a hushed silence fell. The lecturers looked up at him, some more benevolently than others. The very high-backed faux-leather chairs encased them all, encouraging torpor, or in Magnus's case, an increasing sense of nausea. Dr. Sedley talked at length of his forthcoming sabbatical and how the excellent Dr. Grieve would take over during his absence.

"I am sure that my successor will not disappoint and that I am leaving you in very good hands," Dr. Sedley was saying. The speech was turning out to be overlong and most of those present found their own way to distract themselves against boredom. Professor Thwackum, the head of international relations, who was there by mistake, took out her knitting. Unlike her colleagues who consistently misinterpreted polls on election days, she had correctly anticipated a war in Europe and was knitting jumpers for her nieces and nephews in case of penury. Dr. Coffey kept looking at Daphne's *décolleté*. Being of small stature, he could only do so ineffectually, but this nonetheless kept him busy. Sheena Taylor did not need any form of protection against boredom. She sat open-lipped hanging on Dr. Sedley's every word and beaming at him with the full force of her recently whitened dentition. Daphne looked at the speaker with amused scorn and Professor Lehideux had retreated into his own world, constantly turning his back on his colleagues and muttering to himself in what vaguely sounded like French.

Dr. Sedley continued, "And it is my fervent hope that Dr. Grieve will follow in my footsteps in every way so that you do not even notice my absence." This was too much for Daphne. She kicked Magnus under the table and bent down into her cleavage to repress her convulsive laughter. The various members of the executive team followed Dr. Sedley, summarising their reports as best they could so that the meeting would not extend into dinner-time. Magnus's turn as postgraduate admissions director, not part of the executive team, was coming. Daphne gave him a look of encouragement. He was looking straight ahead of him with a sustained glare. His hands were visibly shaking when he gathered his papers together.

Magnus started with suitably banal statistics about the admission of MA students.

"I am pleased to say that the numbers have seen an increase this year."

Dr. Sedley was looking approvingly, thinking the report was coming to an end.

"I trust," Magnus was saying, "that you will not mind if I now strike an academic note. Our esteemed Professor Ifantidou here has just published an article on motivation and language learning and has found during the course of her research that our international students, and our Chinese students in particular, are extremely motivated to come to our university. Her research has uncovered some rather disturbing facts about why this is the case. These concern our admission procedures. Dr. Grieve as head of internationalisation may be aware of this already, but he has not been in touch with me about it so far."

Dr. Grieve jumped and upset what remained of his cup of tea on the floor.

"Dr. Jones, I think this is hardly the forum," he spluttered, but Magnus, who was used to such interruptions from Dr. Grieve, put his hand out like a policeman stopping traffic.

"I am not finished, Dr. Grieve, and I think the rest of the school will be interested in what I have to say. Now to be clear, I need to go through the various stages which characterise our admission procedures in relation to our international students. The first stage consists in me reviewing the students' application documents in my capacity as admissions officer. Whenever applicants have not reached the required grade in the accredited 'International English Language Examination,' I reject them, as indeed I should. However, when in the second stage of the procedure I send the application forms of the rejected applicants back to the administrators, my rejection is ignored, and an offer of a place is made regardless to the students I have just turned down."

Magnus here took a pregnant pause amid hushed comments and a few gasps of shock from various colleagues.

"Now, if I may continue, the administrator's offer of a place is conditional on attending a two months' intensive English language learning course at our Language Centre here at Paine Anglia University. You may think, and you would be justified in thinking, that at the end of the two months' course, the students concerned are asked to retake the accredited 'International English Language Examination' and are sent back to their home university if they fail to make the grade required by our university. But this is not what actually happens. After attending their two months' intensive English language course, the students I rejected just take an internal language test set up by the University Language Centre which no student has ever been known to fail. Then the students I originally rejected simply turn up on our MA programmes, like the proverbial boomerang. Needless to say that many of them go on to fail as they do not have the language resources required to cope with the demands of study at MA level."

Here, Magnus paused again and took a sip from a glass of water Daphne had positioned next to him.

"Ladies and gentlemen, I am very sorry for taking your time over this, but it seems to me that the practice I have just outlined not only makes a mockery of my post as postgraduate admissions officer, but also renders our work teaching and supporting international students much less rewarding than it should be."

Magnus sat down in stunned silence. Everyone knew that something momentous had happened. Inquisitive stares went in the direction of Daphne who tried not to look triumphant.

"Thank you, Dr. Jones, for your oral report," said Dr. Sedley. "I am gratified by the increase in the MA applications you have recorded, and I look forward to receiving your written report tomorrow. You will, of course, omit the reference to the research findings about the admissions procedures you have just communicated to us. I am sure you are aware that they are not appropriate in the context of an administrative report of this kind."

"I am sorry this is what you think," said Magnus, his voice growing steadier and more authoritative, "but I shall not make any changes whatsoever to the report you have just heard, and you shall, therefore, receive it in its entirety."

"I am speechless," said Dr. Sedley. "There will be consequences to this."

Magnus sat down again, and Daphne turned to him saying that he was magnificent. Magnus got up, smiled at her awkwardly, and abruptly left the room to pour himself a strong cup of coffee from the urn in the common room. A few minutes later, several people went up to him to sympathise and congratulate him. Daphne joined them and hugged Magnus.

"Isn't he just wonderful?" she said to whoever was within earshot. "Simply magnificent!"

"I am sorry, Daphne," said Magnus, disengaging himself, "I really must go now."

Magnus ran out of the registry building to the car park, climbed into Gwendolen, and sank into its soft cushions, gasping with exhaustion.

CHAPTER VI

A few days passed. Dr. Adam Grieve moved into Dr. Sedley's office as the acting head of school. This was planned for him to settle in before the Easter break. Physically, Dr. Grieve stood in stark contrast to Dr. Sedley. He was a tall, gaunt-looking man who was so light on his feet that he seemed to glide rather than walk. He had spent much of his life assiduously devoting himself to outward respectability.

He had been fêted by the research community at PAU when he published his supposedly groundbreaking article on Guernsey French, but his statistics were soon found to have been massaged, and rather than defend the indefensible, he let his interest in academic research wane to the point of indifference. In any case, one could get on in academia, and especially at PAU, without being a researcher and at his own request he was placed on a teaching-only contract. He was, soon thereafter and much to his gratification, promoted to the post of Director of Internationalisation on the executive team, which basically consisted in attracting an ever-increasing number of high-fee-paying international students to PAU, a lucrative business for the university as well as a career success for him.

Now that he was entrusted with the running of the department amid the unregulated restlessness of university life, he relished the prospect of a thoroughly Machiavellian period in office. With the help of Professor Lehideux and Dr. Sedley, as well as a battalion of little foot soldiers ever ready to collaborate in this sort of thing, he had already identified the colleagues he would favour and those in whose way he would put obstacles, effecting promotions and demotions, as the occasion required.

This, it must be said, also greatly made up for his ordered home life where for some years now he had been in a companionship with a Bavarian wife rather than in the proper married state. Wedded in their thirties, they had shared similar opinions on all sorts of subjects, including religion and the state of contemporary politics. This, they thought, was enough to enter into a relationship that would survive the passage of time. And it had survived. They had not felt particularly attracted to each other in the early days of their courtship. They tried sex once during their honeymoon, perfunctorily, as something one is expected to do. They did not much like it and decided to give it up as a bad job.

Mrs. Grieve had spent most of her childhood in a single-sex Catholic convent and shared her bed with other girls during the holidays. She was most put out that her husband kept kicking her with his bony knees and ankles during her sleep.

"I wish you'd keep your knees to yourself," she said one day, "I much prefer the soft touch of girls, if you must know."

As for Dr. Grieve, the newness of the occasion had not much aroused him either and he yearned for more room in his bed. It was not long before they decided by common agreement to sleep in different rooms, and that seemed to put an end to any thought of conjugal obligation on either side.

Childless, because children are the result of an intimacy which was never quite achieved, but tolerably happy in their companionship, they inexplicably drifted apart. Mrs. Grieve, who had been an alto at her convent and had gained a reputation for her low singing voice, joined the local female choir. She enjoyed the greater part of the summer touring round Europe with the girl choristers. Dr. Grieve, who was never happier than when he repaired old, clapped-out violins with rabbit glue in the summer house specially designed for this at the bottom of the garden, also spent his holidays apart from Mrs. Grieve, looking for antique violins in French *brocantes* and German *Trödellmarkts*. Once though, they accidentally, and to their great surprise, bumped into each other in the streets of Heidelberg, not that this led to an emotional reunion as they each had booked rooms in different hotels.

As he entered Dr. Sedley's office, Dr. Grieve felt he had stepped into the world of the great and the good, the holy of holies.

"By God, I am happy!" he said to himself.

He was impressed anew at how large the office was, at least three times the size of his own. In the middle of the room stood a round table for meetings with the people who mattered in the university. At the back of the office was an imposing desk made of mahogany. It was so large that it had to curve round the room. Dr. Grieve sat down at it, giving it a light touch of the hand. The desire for sensual pleasure, which is often the only motive for our deeds, was absent in his life, and so another kind of pleasure replaced it, that of cultural capital and the power over others it provided: a large desk in an imposing office would do for now.

The first thing that Dr. Grieve had been instructed to do by his predecessor was to write a letter to that upstart Dr. Jones who would not do as he was told. Dr. Grieve had brought his special Mont Blanc ink pen for the job. He carefully dipped it in the ink bottle by his side. It would be a traditional handwritten message on letter-headed PAU note paper. The letter was as follows:

> *Dear Dr. Jones,*
>
> *I am writing to you to let you know that your responsibility as "postgraduate admission officer" has been taken away from you by the head of school, Dr. Sedley, this day with immediate effect. This is because you have generally been found to be unable to carry out your administrative duties in the appropriate manner and have, in particular, failed to submit the postgraduate admission report in the format required by your line manager, Dr. Sedley.*
>
> *As Head of Internationalisation, I have been asked to take over the post of admission officer from you temporarily until such time as a suitable replacement can be found. I will amend the postgraduate admission report you have submitted so that it conforms to the conventions required by the university regulations and does not include irrelevant material related to academic research.*

Dr. Sedley also informs me that you will need to be allocated more teaching to compensate for the lack of administrative duties. In this respect, we would like you to teach Professor Lehideux's final-year translation seminar after the Easter break. He will be in touch with you concerning the choice of texts to be translated, etc.

Finally, I would like to add that your recent actions will undoubtedly have consequences as far as the completion of your probationary period of employment is concerned with a view to obtaining a permanent position at this university. The outcome of the probationary committee's decision will be communicated to you on your return from the Easter vacation.

Yours ever,
Dr. Adam Grieve.
(Acting Head of School)

Dr. Grieve, as he penned the last words "Acting Head of School," felt such a sudden rush of pleasure as he had not experienced for a long time. His hand, as he dipped his pen into the ink bottle, quivered uncontrollably, and ink spattered onto the desk forming a small puddle. Dr. Grieve quickly used the blotting paper by his side to wipe away the stain. As he looked again, he noticed that the black ink had seeped into areas of the desk where the wood was porous and formed a stain in a shape that looked like a cross. At first, the cross could hardly be seen, but as he rubbed it in an effort to get rid of it altogether, it became more visible. Dr. Grieve rubbed it with even more force, but every time he did so, the cross appeared shinier than ever before, as if it had been inserted into the wood like the inlay of some skilful marquetry. With some more rubbing, it began to look, much to Dr. Grieve's horror, like a crucifix.

Dr. Grieve shakily put the letter in an envelope, sealed it, and rushed out of Dr. Sedley's office to the staff pigeonholes. On his way, he met Daphne, but barely acknowledged her, looking as if he had just seen an apparition.

He located Dr. Jones' letter box. The label on it read: "JONES, Magnus." This reminded him of Professor Lehideux, who, in a fit of fervent republicanism, had insisted that all titles should be removed from the staff pigeonholes and that names should appear in strict alphabetical order, surname first, in French administrative style. Dr. Coffey had said he didn't see why they had to conform to the ways of French bureaucracy, but Professor Lehideux had got his way, nonetheless. The scheme was not extended throughout the university, much as Lehideux had hoped. It simply didn't get past the professor of English literature, Dr. Gardiner, who was reported to have said: "France? All bad ideas come from there!"

Back in Dr. Sedley's office, Dr. Grieve noticed with a great deal of relief that the cross was no longer visible. "The ink must have dried up in the wood, and anyway, I probably imagined the whole thing," he said to himself. He must definitely go and eat something; you don't half hallucinate on an empty stomach!

And so, like the majority of us when confronted with a sign, Dr. Grieve attributed it to a material phenomenon, his digestion. We are afforded moments, all of us, to reflect on how we persecute others, but we choose instead to reduce them to a chemical imbalance or a mere hallucination.

CHAPTER VII

The Easter break beckoned and with it a much-awaited picnic on Holkham Beach. Magnus had been meeting Henrietta more frequently in the last few days. Lady Agatha seemed to get on well enough with her. A diminutive, vivacious, doll-like woman in her twenties, Henrietta Gillespie was excessively fond of her naturally heart-shaped lips which she highlighted with vivid red lipstick. As a chartered accountant, she had been entrusted with auditing the accounts of the family firm, and very actively attended the monthly board meetings with Aled and Lady Agatha, the main shareholders.

Lady Agatha had initially been disappointed that Henrietta's only claim to aristocratic connections was a short period of work in the Royal Household. Nonetheless, Henrietta made as much of that as she possibly could. On first entering Holton Hall, she had exclaimed that the entrance reminded her exactly of Sandringham.

"Much more modest, of course," she said, "but the proportions are exactly the same, oh, and these rugs, quite the same pattern as the ones in the Queen's drawing room."

The garrulous flow of analogies had not much impressed Lady Agatha, but she was prepared to let it go on account of nervousness and youthful enthusiasm.

As the day was looking fine, they decided to go to Holkham Beach for a picnic in the dunes. Magnus directed the whole party, driving between Holton Hall and the rectory and picking up Lady Agatha, the children, Aled, and Isabella. Everybody was punctual. Rev. Bold, who was awfully keen to show off his newly acquired electric car, offered a lift to Alessandro and Henrietta. Alessandro declined the invitation as he was to drive the horse box, but Henrietta, who had been told about the merits of the vehicle in minute details and was not particularly fond of the smell of horses, very readily accepted it.

Holkham Beach could do nothing but draw admiration from everyone on first arriving. It was a wide expanse of sand bordered by moderately sized dunes and an odorous pine forest affording shady relief from the persistent Norfolk sun. Despite the scenery, the picnic first had a dullness which Magnus found difficult to overcome.

When they all sat down, Henrietta turned much of her attention to Aled, laughing at his jokes and ignoring everybody else. Magnus had never seen her so lively and in her desire to please she was in danger of losing some of the genteel veneer she had perfected as second nature to her. Aled had a gift for anecdotes and every story he told of Holton Hall, the farm, and his tenants was met with excitement, Henrietta urging him on flirtatiously. Although Magnus did not harbour any feelings of jealousy for his elder brother, this obvious preferment did not escape his notice. He had wondered about Henrietta's feelings for him and the more he saw of her, the more he wondered if he would be happy with her, were he to propose to her. He liked her well enough as a friend, and found her very attractive indeed, but there was something, he could not exactly pinpoint what, which he found off-putting in her. He had not mentioned this to his mother, yet, but for the moment, the only thing that could happen between them was a flirtation, and even that, by the looks of it, seemed highly unlikely.

Things got livelier when Lady Agatha, noticing that the party was a little subdued, started to unpack the food from the picnic basket, laying it out carefully on the rug.

"And of course, there's 'Mrs. Church' unpasteurised cheese!" she said, hoping to rouse the others from the torpor in which they had fallen. "Our very own cheese made from our Guernsey cows' raw milk," she added, offering the first chunk to Henrietta.

"Oh, no, I couldn't possibly," said Henrietta, "I never eat unpasteurised cheese."

Lady Agatha gave ever so slight a snort and offered the cheese to Alessandro instead. This was not made any better by Rev. Bold who said, wringing his hands in an ingratiating kind of way, that he'd brought his own vegan picnic food and Miss Gillespie was very welcome to it. There was no cheese in sight, but gluten-free bread, some almond drink, and a few ripe avocadoes to share around. His address was chiefly to Henrietta and she said, in reply:

"Thank you very much indeed. I think I may be becoming lactose intolerant so the almond milk will do nicely."

"Good, glad to be of help; some people may eat anything, you know," the curate said, looking at Lady Agatha, "but I thought you were one of the discerning ecological kind."

"And where do your avocadoes come from then, eh, Reverend Bold?" asked Aled, keeping his tone as jovial and free of irritation as he possibly could, given the circumstances.

Rev. Bold, after inspecting the label stuck on the dark brown skin of his fruit, reluctantly admitted that it came from Peru.

Whilst Rev. Bold and Henrietta sat apart in vegan aloofness, the Jones family and Alessandro heartily ate the cheese. The language of this story would fail in its adjectives to describe it. It filled the mouth with the soft goodness of creamy Guernsey milk. It mingled, as Somerset Maugham says of punch, the vagueness of music and the precision of mathematics; it had the warmth of a good heart. One felt the cheese had been made with the sole purpose of doing one a good turn.

"It's famously good," said Magnus biting into another chunk and winking at his brother. "I've seen it in all the local shops; it's doing well."

"And long may that continue," said Aled. "We need to produce more food in this crowded country of ours."

"I'm very glad to hear of its success," observed Lady Agatha with a note of melancholy in her voice, "all is not lost then."

Magnus looked at his watch.

"Oh, I say," he said, "we should be getting the horses. Are you ready, Henrietta?"

"Oh, you go riding with your brother," said Henrietta piqued at the direction the conversation had taken. She had only ridden once at Sandringham and still felt quite inexperienced even though the riding there was naturally superlative.

"But I've got Mummy's mare out especially for you. You'll love her. She's very gentle."

Henrietta after a few more protestations finally agreed to come along. Reverend Bold, who had never ridden before, said he didn't intend to until horses were bred with much shorter legs. Everyone laughed and said that surely that meant he could ride poneys upon which he declared that he would be very happy just paddling on the beach and, turning to look at Alessandro, that anyone was welcome to join him in this harmless activity. Alessandro, who did not particularly want to be forming a threesome with Henrietta and Magnus, rose to his feet and said he'd be happy to join Rev. Bold.

"I thought you were coming with us to help with the horses," said Magnus, taken aback by Alessandro's sudden alacrity to be with the curate.

"You'll manage without me, I daresay. I think I'll go for a swim while I'm at it."

"A swim at this time of year!" said Isabella. "That is brave!"

"Sandro is tough, make no mistake!" said Magnus who for some inexplicable reason to himself was relieved that Alessandro was not going to be paddling with the insufferable vicar.

"We'll meet up on the shore," he said, pointing to the water's edge some distance away from the dunes where they were sitting.

"Actually, I have to come with you," said Alessandro. "I left my swimming trunks in the car."

Magnus, Henrietta, and Alessandro walking behind them left the company and walked towards the avenue of trees where the horse box was parked. As Alessandro had predicted, Magnus and Henrietta exchanged pleasantries and ignored him.

"You nearly caught it, there, you know," said Magnus jokingly.

"You mean about the cheese?"

"Yes, well, we have different views. Welcome to the twenty-first century! We can embrace different ways of living, can't we? And as long as one does not encroach on the other, I'm fine with it. I get too much encroachment at work. I'm thinking of resuming my training as a vicar."

After a short moment of silence, Henrietta began with, "A vicar! I must say I am very surprised about this."

"Why should you be surprised? My training wasn't very successful first time round, but I've grown older and the call to serve God is still there. Is there something objectionable to being a vicar?"

"I couldn't be more against it, not least the fact that you're a respected academic and to go from that to a dead-end career seems such a waste."

"I say, what about a bishop then?" said Magnus, trying to make light of things.

"There aren't many of them, are there?"

"So you think the work of a vicar which is to look after his parishioners' salvation in this and the other world a worthless activity?"

"If you put it like this and you believe in what you're doing, I suppose it must feel like an important vocation, but since I have no such belief in a world other than this one, I'm afraid I cannot agree with you as to the importance of being a mere country vicar."

"A mere country vicar! Henrietta, have you seen how vicars are called upon to preside over the most important moments of village life temporally and eternally, its births, its marriages, and its deaths? Doesn't that mean more than all the honours and accolades I may get in academia?"

"You attribute more importance to your vocation than is perceived by contemporary society. You think you can use religion to exert power over people, don't you? And that's wrong."

"I do not see training for ordination as in any way a matter of power over people, but by keeping the faith and doing things that seem little and insignificant, vicars can demonstrate the love

God has for all his children, irrespective of whether they are Jews or Greek, slave or free, male or female. Remember what St. Paul said?"

"Indeed, we do, or at least we should do," said Alessandro gently, no longer being able to stay silent.

"There you have it," cried Henrietta. "You already have one convert, but why did you give up on ordination in the first place?"

This brought back painful memories which Magnus had no intention to disclose to Henrietta.

"Hang it all!" he said. "The sea beckons and so do the horses!"

Luckily, it was time to deliver the horses from their airless box and they were in very high spirits. Magnus's horse belonged to his brother Aled, but they shared him for occasions such as this. Lucinda, Lady Agatha's light brown mare, was used to being ridden by Isabella who adored her gentle nature. Lady Agatha had had Lucinda ever since she was a filly, and years of propinquity had allowed for a close relationship to develop between the two. One touch from Lady Agatha would calm Lucinda even if she were seriously spooked. Magnus, too, had a special way with horses, and despite the initial excitement, they let him lead them calmly to the path leading to the beach. Magnus helped Henrietta onto the mare, and they set off in a pleasant walk towards the beach. Alessandro had quickly changed into his swimming shorts and said he'd sprint to the shore. He was a fast runner, and he soon overtook them. Henrietta held herself rigidly and ungainly on her mount. Magnus advised her to relax a little, but she said she did not want to look as if she were sagging.

As they approached the water's edge, the horses broke into a trot ever so more gaily splashing in the water. They could see Rev. Bold with his trousers rolled up paddling in the distance and decided they'd gallop towards him. Magnus relished the feeling of his horse lunging forward. With his smooth long stride, it was like riding on the crest of a wave. Henrietta was not doing quite so well. When Magnus looked back, he realised that Lucinda had refused to go into a gallop. Both rider and mount eventually caught up with him, but for some reason, the mare would not stop and slowly clip-clopped away from the shore into the water.

"Where is she going?" screamed Henrietta. "Where the hell is she going?"

"Turn her around," said Magnus, "and she'll soon come round."

But no amount of pulling on the reins, or indeed frantic kicking, would do it. The mare kept going until the water met with her flanks. Then, with a snort, not unlike that of Lady Agatha, the obstinate mare simply sat down in the waves bringing Henrietta down with her. Henrietta gave a desperate scream but had the presence of mind to jump off the horse and swim away from her. As there was practically no depth, she walked the rest of the way and met Magnus who had come to rescue her.

"That bloody stupid mare," cried a drenched Henrietta, her mass of hair now hanging limply round her face, much to Alessandro's amusement. "What are you smirking at?" she said angrily. "It's not funny." Then deciding it was better to laugh with the others than being laughed at, she broke into what sounded halfway between laughter and a scream.

"You weren't scared, were you?" asked Magnus.

"There, have my towel," said Alessandro.

Magnus clicked his tongue and with a swoosh, the mare presently came ashore. He walked with both horses on each side of him. They passed Rev. Bold who had seen the whole thing and smiled sympathetically at Henrietta.

"You'd better come in my car, what with it being electric the heating is very efficient and will dry you up in no time."

Henrietta was to travel back with Magnus in the camper van but even he agreed that Rev. Bold's car was a preferable alternative.

"Reverend Bold's right, my camper van is very draughty; you have more of a chance of drying up in his car."

They soon reached Gwendolen in which the family and the children were waiting making cups of hot tea and eating the scones Aled had baked in the morning before the picnic. Henrietta and

Reverend Bold turned away without so much as a wave goodbye. Soon the electric car vanished, whirring out of sight.

Magnus was vexed almost beyond what he could hide from the others. He was most struck by the indifference of Henrietta leaving without even a word of gratitude of common kindness to his family. How could she be so self-regarding about everything? He thought again of the cheese incident, and as he turned to meet everybody, he could read his mother's disappointment. He looked at Alessandro who was slowly but expertly manoeuvring the horse box. He wound down his window.

"Do you want to come over for a meal at the rectory this evening? I've got a new CD of *Winterreise* I'd like to listen to. Shall we listen to it together?"

Winterreise and a bottle of wine sounded like a very pleasant proposition. An evening of eating, drinking, and listening to classical music in Alessandro's company seemed, after the wretched Holkham Beach scheme, like pure felicity.

CHAPTER VIII

Magnus was cooking *cawl*, the Welsh soup he'd seen his father make when he was a child. The rich smell of lamb stewing in the oven never failed to bring back happy memories; he could hear his father's lilting voice, telling him to cook the vegetables separately to give them more taste. Magnus had but a superficial knowledge of Welsh, but his father's approbation, "da iawn ti," meant more to him than a mere "well done you." The trick of his father's voice, long gone, had survived in him.

As he went on cooking, Magnus reflected on the awfulness of the Holkham Beach picnic. He wondered what the others made of it. Why had he carried on talking to Henrietta when she made disparaging comments about his calling to be a vicar? He'd ignored Alessandro. The recollection made him redden with guilt. It had been an afternoon more devoid of pleasure than any other he had spent. A whole evening of music with Alessandro would be sheer joy compared to it. Magnus felt he had been negligent of his friend's constant care of him. But it should be so no more. They were going away to the Peak District and would have a ripping time, just like in the old days.

The phone rang. It was Alessandro. He couldn't make this evening. He had to wait for his mother's call on the landline; she was ill and he may have to go back to Sicily. He hoped it would not clash with their trip to Derbyshire, but it may have to. He was sorry.

"Not to worry, there'll be other times," said Magnus, keen to disguise the note of disappointment in his voice.

"I'll try to go to Sicily after our trip, but you know how it is sometimes with my mother."

"It's all right. Really, don't let it worry you, Sandro."

Magnus put the phone down, crestfallen. The *cawl* would be eaten in solitude with none of the playful conversation that came with Alessandro's company. It was a melancholy change for the long evening ahead of him. Magnus sighed over it and wished for what may be impossible: a week's holiday with Alessandro walking in the lusciously green hills of Derbyshire. He tried to cheer himself up by reading *Emma* for his next seminar. For a brief moment, he fancied himself as a "Mr. Knightley" to Alessandro, giving him necessary admonitions and faithful counsel. He smiled at the thought, ridiculous as it was. Still, the evening was suddenly more bearable. Maybe that's why copies of Jane Austen were given to soldiers in the trenches.

The next day, Magnus decided to travel to PAU. The car park was nearly empty as the students were away from the university, but Magnus, who had by now been banned from using it, had taken to parking in side streets near campus. His old Cambridge bike fitted perfectly at the back of Gwendolen. He relished cycling to his classes, feeling like an old don, his college scarf flying in the wind. Students and colleagues would inquire if he'd cycled all the way from North Norfolk. Some days, he'd cycle next to young Dr. Coffey. It was difficult to keep up with him and look elegant at the same time. Dr. Coffey's was a different, less sedate, style of cycling. His Lycra shorts accentuated the shape of his muscular buttocks, and Magnus was strangely impressed by them.

One of the reasons why he was coming into work this morning was that Dr. Grieve, realising that his message, painstakingly written on letter-headed paper, had not reached Magnus, had summoned him to a meeting by email. Just before the meeting, Magnus walked past the egalitarian pigeonholes, but did not open his.

He knocked on the door. Dr. Grieve said to come in. He had acquired all the mannerisms of importance, sitting at his imposing desk with an ungracious air. Magnus was determined to make no effort for pleasant conversation with a man who seemed so intent on being disagreeable.

As soon as Magnus sat down, Dr. Grieve began in the following manner:

"You can be at no loss, Magnus, to understand the reason of my calling you here."

Magnus looked with calm surprise; then words came flowing out, sarcastically eloquent.

"Absolutely, Dr. Grieve, I've not been able to account for the honour you bestow upon me by summoning me to this august office of yours."

"Magnus," replied Dr. Grieve in an angry tone of voice, "you should understand that I am not in a mood to be mocked. But however whimsical you may choose to be, you will not find me so. I am known for my frankness and my integrity and so I shall go straight to the point. I must inform you that the promotion committee have decided to extend your probationary period for another year. As no doubt you are aware, this means that your post is still not permanent and that you will have to reapply for it next year. I must also point out that there is no appeal against our decision which was arrived at mainly because your administrative abilities have been found wanting since your appointment. We need to see evidence that they will improve in the coming year."

"I am not clear in what respect I have been found wanting," said Magnus, colouring with astonishment.

"For one, it may be an idea for you to take more care over the way you fill in your promotion forms in the future. The committee found that you did not provide sufficient information in your submission. You used bullet points for most sections; it was obviously a rushed job."

"But you advised me not to spend too much time on the form and to use bullet points, since in your own words I had nothing to worry about."

"Did I say that? Someone of your calibre with a Cambridge PhD and you can't even fill in a form. I mean, really. There is also the small matter of the postgraduate admissions tutor's report which I had to rewrite myself in the appropriate format."

"You mean you suppressed it."

"Your so-called revelations were unfounded and would have reflected badly on our university. They were best taken out."

"I don't think Professor Ifantifou would like to hear her research findings being referred to as unfounded revelations. I consider this to be a setup from beginning to end."

"I really don't see why I should be putting up with this sort of language. Now do you have anything else to say?"

"Only this: as far as I am concerned, the promotion committee, being constituted of people like you, has no legitimacy whatsoever. You will not succeed in intimidating me."

Dr. Grieve hesitated for a moment and then replied:

"I thought you may be more willing to cooperate. But I am not all that surprised. I have just heard that you've been banned from using the university's car park for parking inappropriately. I am beginning to build a picture of you as someone who has a problem with authority."

"Only with those who claim to have it when they plainly do not. I leave this to your conscience."

Dr. Grieve reddened. The black inky cross seemed to swim again into his vision, and he gripped the desk with such force that his knuckles whitened.

"You're a headstrong man. I've had it with your constant talk of conscience. I am shocked and astonished. But do not be deceived that we shall ever want to promote you at this university."

"Your threats do not intimidate me in the slightest, Dr. Grieve. I'm hardly surprised you don't like my talk of conscience. The way people are rewarded in this institution for jumping on vacuous bandwagons rather than actually doing their jobs as academics is downright scandalous. I now have colleagues in so-called 'authority' above me who have not got so much as a PhD. I wonder how long this university can survive before students wise up to what a sham it all is and stop coming to us."

"Be that as it may, we have allocated you more teaching to make up for your loss of administrative responsibilities. Professor Lehideux has agreed to let you take over from his translation class as from the start of the summer term. He will contact you about the texts that you should be using for translation."

"I can expect nothing better from you. I will happily take on the extra load if only to save students from Lehideux's teaching, but I will under no circumstances accept his advice concerning the choice of translation texts. Once the module is mine to organise, I consider myself free to teach whatever I think is appropriate for the students under my guidance."

"Words fail me at your arrogance. But again do not deceive yourself that we shall ever want to give you a permanent position in this university!"

"I have no illusions on that score and you can now have nothing further to say. You and your acolytes have insulted me in any which way you thought possible. I must now leave and consider my options."

And he rose as he spoke. Dr. Grieve rose also and Magnus proceeded to leave the room.

"You seem to have no regard for the reputation of this university. Don't you consider that your revelations about our admissions procedures may have injured us all?"

"Dr. Grieve, I have said all I needed to say. You know my feelings on the matter. The reputation of the university has no claim on me whatsoever in the present circumstances."

"Then, all I can say to you is that I am seriously disappointed in you," Dr. Grieve limply concluded.

Magnus did not answer and walked out of the office, silently closing the door behind him. He sighed what must be a sigh of relief. Daphne was waiting outside waving a piece of paper around in an agitated manner.

"What were you in there for? Is anything the matter?"

"Somewhat predictably, I have had my post as admissions tutor taken away from me and I am still on probation for another year."

Daphne emitted a little scream and burst out into peals of laughter.

"You will get your permanent post all right within days when he finds out what I've got there," she said, brandishing the piece of paper once more.

"What is it?"

"A copy of an email Professor Lehideux sent to Dr. Grieve and Dr. Sedley. In it, he advises them to keep a log of all your administrative failings and to encourage my students to speak out against my teaching methods."

"How on earth did you get hold of this?"

"The silly fool sent the email to me by mistake! All I could think on first reading this stuff was why am I being mentioned in this message in the third person? Then it all dawned on me, and made me very angry that they were ganging up against us in that way. Talk of administrative failings. This is the biggest administrative failing of them all!" she said, marching into Dr. Grieve's office without so much as bothering to knock.

Magnus heard raised voices. Daphne's was particularly loud. He smiled. He was happy, still looking forward to the Derbyshire trip. Alessandro would wangle it somehow. A trip in Gwendolen would erase all the unhappiness of work. Daphne came out looking triumphant.

"I've contacted the union. They're taking this on. I've been advised to take Professor Lehideux to court or at the very least get a formal apology from him. It won't be long before you get your permanent post, I can guarantee it."

At that moment, Dr. Grieve opened the door looking as pale as a sheet. He was sure the cross of Jesus had hovered into view again, and there was no way he was going to stay in that office one more minute.

"The man looks as if he's had a vision," said Magnus.

"You bet he has," said Daphne, "the vision of his forced resignation. Once I hold a rat, I'm like a ferret: I don't let go of it."

CHAPTER IX

As Magnus got into Gwendolen, a feeling of melancholy reigned over him—it wasn't clear he'd be going away with Alessandro during the Easter break after all, and the sad business at PAU had been a depressing spectacle of human imperfections, but as he drove on, his mood cleared; the sight of the daffodils in the grassy verges lifted him up. He remembered Wordsworth's line that one could not but be "gay in such a jocund company." This made him smile not least about how words evolve to acquire impossibly different meanings.

He finally got to Holton and pulled up on the drive at the rectory only to find Rev. Bold's electric car parked there and Rev. Bold inside it. The curate jumped out eagerly walking towards Magnus.

"Well, Dr. Jones," cried Rev. Bold, "isn't this the most momentous news?"

"What news?" replied Magnus, unable to understand what the curate was so excited about.

"About Alessandro's mother. Her illness was a false alarm after all and Alessandro is no longer needed in Sicily, at least for the time being. I've just met him and he told me to mention it to you if I saw you before he did."

"So what did he say?" asked Magnus, surprised that the Rev. should be the bearer of such a message, however pleasing it was.

"He told me about how you were all set to go to Derbyshire."

The curate's behaviour was so agitated that Magnus did not know how to understand it. The character of the man seemed preposterously altered.

"I came here the moment I found out to make a suggestion to you," said Rev. Bold. "Let me explain. Do you remember that time on Holkham Beach when Alessandro offered to join me in paddling along the shore? We exchanged such glances on that occasion that I have thought about it ever since. He and I paddling together; such a precious moment. And this is what I've really come to see you about. I have a little cottage in Matlock in the Peak District, you see, a bolt-hole, a love nest, some would call it. And well, I have invited Alessandro to stay there with me this Easter break."

"And has he accepted your invitation?"

"He did mention the fact that he had a previous engagement with you, but we thought, seeing as you're just friends, that you wouldn't mind postponing your trip with him. Are you with me?"

Magnus's eyes were immediately averted. He detested the vulgarity of the cliché and remained silent for what seemed to Rev. Bold a very long time.

"I'm afraid I can't give you an answer, Rev. Bold, until I have spoken to Alessandro myself," he said in the determined, steady kind of voice that should have brought the interaction to an end.

Yet, he had to listen once more to Rev. Bold's fervent, if deficient, narrative about the many circumstances in which Alessandro had shown favour towards him, how that day he would liked to take him to tea in his electric car and had to suffer a very wet Henrietta instead, and how Alessandro would have graced him by his presence . . .

Magnus was at that moment experiencing a confusion of emotions and a perplexing intrusion of menacing thoughts towards the curate. He was saved from further rapturous reports by the sound of Rev. Leigh's footsteps. Andrew Bold was in far too nervous a state to meet him—he "had better go"—and much to Magnus's relief, he jumped into his car with as much alacrity as he'd jumped out of it, waving goodbye at Magnus and at a bemused Rev. Leigh.

"Seems in a bit of a hurry," said Rev. Leigh archly. "I was coming about the readings this coming Sunday. Are you able to do one of them, Magnus?"

"Sorry, I think I mentioned it to you a while back, but I should have done so again. I'm going away on a trip to Derbyshire with Alessandro this coming weekend so I won't be in church."

"Anywhere nice?" inquired the vicar.

"Matlock, I think," said Magnus.

The moment the vicar was gone, Magnus was able to give vent to his feelings. Good God! How that insufferable curate with his half-baked ideas could ever have had the presumption to raise his interest to Alessandro! But surely Alessandro would not return Rev. Bold's affections. Magnus's suspicions were allayed when he remembered Alessandro had called Andrew Bold a foolish man. But they had clearly shown particular notice to each other on two separate occasions: on Mother's Day when Alessandro had bashfully returned with a bunch of daffodils, and on Holkham Beach when Alessandro had shown some eagerness to join the curate in paddling by the shore. These were the only two times witnessed by Magnus, but there may well have been others. Still, the feelings occasioned by this brooding were surely too negative. Circumstances which seemed to indicate the curate's affection for Alessandro were too apt to swell disproportionately in Magnus's mind.

In any case, how could he have such proprietary feelings for Alessandro when he was not even attracted to him? His earliest memories of being romantically involved related to women. He had often thought of his dream woman. Falling in love with her in Hyde Park, his eyes fell on her strolling up to the Serpentine and sitting down at the café looking out on it. She was petite, blonde, and pretty with eyes so blue that the light reflected in them like the water of the lake in front of them. She turned to him. They stared at each other forgetting where they were. He spoke to her.

"You've been waiting for me like the other half of me."

"At last, you've come," she whispered.

"Let's go somewhere," he said to her.

They caught a night ferry to Calais and slept outside on the deck in the star-studded night.

He thought of his old daydream and it seemed even more ridiculous that he should now be jealous of Rev. Bold. This jealousy must be disordered and devilishly imposed upon him. Alessandro was a man, had all the characteristics of manhood, even if he was angelic. But then he was a man, too. Whatever Alessandro had, he had also. Nothing "other" there. He started thinking of sharing his body with Alessandro's and there was no repulsion. There was just immense respect and affection. It would be like making love to one's own self, knowing precisely what to expect.

Did his feelings replace those he had for Henrietta? He compared the two and saw that Alessandro occupied an immensely superior place in his affection than Henrietta ever could. The truth was that compared to his feelings for Alessandro, he had never loved her at all. And yet, he had been aroused by her in a way that he could never have been by Alessandro.

Now that he had examined his heart in this piecemeal, almost declarative way, now what? There was still the abhorrent possibility of Bold spending the Easter break with Alessandro. The attraction was certainly there. Yet the very thought of it disgusted Magnus. How could Alessandro debase himself to a union with a man so clearly his inferior? How could it be? It was impossible. And yet, it was possible. The incongruity of his own feelings rendered Bold's attachment to his friend all the more possible.

The question kept gnawing at his conscience: how could he be so affected by Rev. Bold's interest in Alessandro?

In an instant, his heart opened itself to him and his eyes filled with tears: he was, inexplicably, in love with Alessandro. Further analyses were not necessary for this was now a certainty, and one to which his heart assented fully and steadfastly: he was in love with Alessandro.

There with his spirits refreshed, he took a turn in the rectory garden, smelling the odorous broom, and cutting off a few flowers with which to make a bouquet when he saw Alessandro passing through the gate at the bottom of the garden and coming towards him.

This was the first time they'd seen each other since Alessandro's disappointing phone call that he may have to return to Sicily. Magnus had been cutting daffodils, thinking of Alessandro and gay and jocund company; there was not much time for composure of mind.

CHAPTER X

Alessandro walked up the gravel path; there was but a minute before they were together. In that minute, Magnus's mind was resolved. He had for many years been Alessandro's best friend. Of that he was sure. Alessandro had cared for him, watched over him when he was ill, tucked him up in bed and brought him hot drinks when he was shivering. In spite of all this, Magnus had often been inattentive and interested in women he soon grew tired of. He knew he was dear to Alessandro.

Then, they were together, Alessandro standing awkwardly before him. He joked that this time, it was Magnus holding a bunch of daffodils. This brought back the painful recollection in Magnus's mind of Rev. Bold's attachment to his friend. Magnus asked about Alessandro's mother. She was well. It had been a false alarm. Alessandro must be relieved. Yes he was. This was good news. Magnus thought there was apprehension in his friend's voice as if perhaps he was about to communicate Rev. Bold's plan to him.

They walked round the garden looking for more flowers in silence. Alessandro seemed to be looking at him. This brought on another fear. Was he about to tell him that he was going out with Rev. Bold? After a while, Magnus felt the silence to be unbearable. Smiling, he began:

"I have some news which I think will surprise you."

"Have you?" Alessandro said calmly. "Good or bad?"

"Good, the likelihood, the certainty, in fact, of my post being made permanent."

"Excellent news! How is this?"

"Daphne found out that Professor Lehideux was encouraging other colleagues to find fault with us. The fool included her in an email which was intended for Dr. Sedley and Dr. Grieve. Unfortunately for him, the message went into some detail as to how colleagues should compile a list of all our misdemeanours and administrative failings."

"Talk about the biggest administrative failing, sending this to the person concerned. Is there a chance he might lose his post because of this?"

"I doubt it. PAU works in impenetrable ways. He'll probably be moved to another sector of the university and promoted to dean of whatever happens to be flavour of the day."

"Dean of Equity, Diversity, and Inclusion," said Alessandro, "I heard this was popular these days."

"Yes, quite, only at PAU it's bound to be Dean of EDI," said Magnus. "Anyway, I'll just be happy with a formal apology and my post being made permanent. It's Daphne he should be worried about. She's bound to uncover more shenanigans. She should have gone into forensic linguistics; honestly, the way she keeps at it, it's quite remarkable. It's too little too late as far as I am concerned. I don't have the energy. I think I may be changing course. I have been tempted to shout and curse, too, but Daphne does this very well on my behalf. I'm of a quietist disposition. I need to be able to forgive. Hate the sin, but not the sinner and all that."

"Yes, but what if Daphne does uncover any more wrongdoing? Won't you have to be involved?"

"I really don't have the appetite for it."

"I can quite understand. There's neither need for regret nor triumph. These people are a disgrace to academia. To think they may be rewarded with promotion!"

"There is a sickness in our universities. Can you imagine what it must feel like to study in fear of being marked down for expressing views that diverge from the reigning orthodoxy? I had a student come to me the other day saying how much she enjoyed my seminars. This was the first time in her three years at PAU that Christianity had been mentioned positively."

Magnus could say no more about the demise of academia. It was not the topic uppermost on his mind. They seemed to be about to broach the subject of Rev. Bold and Derbyshire, but Magnus's instinct was to avoid it. He'd talk about something different. He inquired about Alessandro's brother, Georgio, and if he'd managed to leave home, yet. Alessandro startled him by saying:

"Oh, I'm free to go to Derbyshire with you next week by the way, if you're still up for it. Have you had time to book a campsite, yet?"

"No, I wasn't sure you could make it."

Magnus thought he may help with Alessandro's confession about his relationship with Rev. Bold, and after a few steps, he said:

"If you have any wish to ask my opinion as a friend about your relationship with Rev. Bold and want to confide in me about it, that is, if you'd rather go with him to Derbyshire, I'm at your command."

"My relationship with Rev. Bold!" repeated Alessandro. "Magnus, what's all this about? There is no such thing. There is at present no other relationship than the one I have with you."

"Rev. Bold came round before you to ask me if we could postpone the trip so that you two could go together instead."

"Magnus, I hope you didn't think for one minute that I'd agreed to such a plan. This is entirely of his own making. I've been looking forward to this trip with you for weeks."

And while he spoke, Magnus was able to discern with relief that Alessandro's attachment to Rev. Bold was a complete delusion. Of course, Magnus felt for Andrew Bold, but he had more of a right to attach Alessandro to himself than anybody else. So what did Magnus say? Just enough to make Alessandro aware of how much his heart was ready to receive him. But nothing in what he said could be anything but vague. There was just an airy, noncommittal understanding between them that nobody, not Andrew Bold, not even Henrietta, could split them apart.

Alessandro had come with the intention of making sure his friend had survived his ordeal at PAU, and to check that he was still free to go with him on a camping trip. He had long given up hope that his friendship with Magnus would ever develop into anything resembling a relationship. He'd been with Magnus when Henrietta was around and he'd known that this was impossible. There had been pangs of jealousy about her and all that she could offer to Magnus which he could not. He remembered that day in Holkham, how he'd humiliated himself by following them, preferring to feel unwanted and ignored than to allow further dalliance between them. No, he had not been indifferent to Magnus, and if this plan of a marriage between Henrietta and his friend failed, he'd be the happiest man on earth. He had rushed to the rectory to see how this sweetest of friends bore all the problems at PAU, and had found him agitated over Rev. Bold. Within half an hour, Alessandro had travelled from a dim awareness of his influence on Magnus to something so much like love that to call it by any other name would be wrong.

As for Magnus, he had gone from an uncertainty of Alessandro's feelings for him to the assurance that he was loved by him and that all would be well. The feelings of rivalry he had harboured towards Andrew Bold had entirely dissipated.

"We shall go to Derbyshire," Alessandro declared, and without knowing why, he hugged his friend and kissed him on the lips. He muttered an apology and walked away quickly.

CHAPTER XI

Magnus had by no means forgotten Alessandro's kiss when he awoke the next morning; but he remembered its touch, more forceful, more substantial than he had ever experienced when kissing women. He had not disliked its roughness because it was Alessandro's kiss, and was no less affected by it than he had been the day before. Alessandro was his by right; this was what he most earnestly wanted.

Having so happily settled this persuasion in his mind, Magnus started on the job of kitting Gwendolen out. The oil level must be checked, the water tank filled up, the little larder supplied with all the requisites for cosy breakfasts, enough crockery and cutlery for two, pots, pans, yes, it was all there. Oh, and he must get Alessandro's favourite raspberry jelly. Alessandro no doubt would bring the delicious almond cakes baked by his aunt in Sicily. He had them in great abundance as they were regularly delivered to the rectory by post, carefully wrapped in cotton tea-towels.

Having finished his preparations, he could not but be surprised to see his mother coming down the path from the hall. Lady Agatha did not usually appear until after her elevenses. Her coming was surely to do with the forthcoming trip.

In his foreboding he had quite forgotten the state of disarray around Gwendolen. There were buckets of water, wet dishcloths, a discarded oil can and a pair of old wellies on the ground. He was standing in the middle of it all looking dishevelled. Lady Agatha surveyed the mess but could not miss the look of boyish excitement that precedes long journeys on Magnus's face.

"Off somewhere then?" she said a little dubiously.

"Yes, Alessandro and I are going to Bakewell tomorrow."

"I thought he was going with Rev. Bold. Henrietta came to tell me this morning. She said Alessandro had cancelled the trip with you. She's up at the hall by the way, waiting to see you."

"News travels fast, but obviously not fast enough. Alessandro came to tell me yesterday evening that Bold's arrangement had been carried out and publicised without his assent. Alessandro and I had planned to go to Derbyshire weeks before Rev. Bold's invitation. We spoke on the subject yesterday, and our plans remain unchanged. We are going to the Peak District. As for Henrietta, I am very busy and will not, indeed cannot, see her at this moment."

There was a start and exclamation on hearing this.

"But I spoke to Henrietta this morning and she tells me that she was invited to Rev. Bold's cottage as well and has accepted it herself. Oh, this is such a muddle!"

"It is very clear to me, Mama, Rev. Bold knew about our previous plans and chose to ignore them. He really should refrain from further unpleasantness. Alessandro and I have come to an understanding that nothing can separate us from each other, least of all Rev. Bold."

"Am I to understand that Alessandro turned down Rev. Bold's invitation?"

"Yes."

"Refused him in fact to go with you instead?"

"Yes."

"On what grounds, if I may ask?"

"Alessandro has no interest in starting a relationship with Rev. Bold, which is what all this was about in the first place."

"I can certainly understand that, but he must have been aware of Rev. Bold favouring him."

"He wishes to ignore it. Alessandro has always been particular to me."

"To you?"

Lady Agatha looked at him with suspicious surprise.

"This is beyond anything I can imagine. You've always been interested in women. How can you possibly return his affection? Anyway, there's nothing more to be said. Henrietta's waiting."

And for a few minutes, Lady Agatha remained silent. Magnus likewise said nothing. He emptied a bucket into the hedge and made out as if he was tidying up the mess around him.

"As you know," said Lady Agatha, beginning again, "I am an advocate of marrying early and was very comforted when your brother married Isabella in his early twenties. I wish you'd been keener to fix yourself in a similar way. Henrietta has been kept waiting for far too long now. Now, have you any reason why this match should not happen?"

"Yes, Mother, I have examined my heart and found it was not ready to receive her. She lacks principles."

"How can you know that?"

"She has allowed secularism and fashionable ideas to take hold over her completely. She was very dismissive of me becoming a vicar."

"Oh, that . . ."

"Yes, that. Spirituality evades her completely. I could not possibly marry such a woman."

"It would have been so good to have your children and Henrietta so ready for that use."

"My love has no use. Alessandro has 'a woman's gentle heart' but not acquainted with shifting change as is false women's fashion."

"Shakespeare."

"'Sonnet 20.'"

"Magnus, for God's sake, Elizabethan love won't do at all here. How could you ever get into that? Literature has addled your brain and, apparently, quite confused you below the belt!"

"Mama, Henrietta could never succeed with me. And I am quite sure that I could never make her happy either, and . . ."

"My dear," interrupted Lady Agatha, "there is no need for this. Your feelings are now as well known to me as my intentions are to you. Let the subject no longer be broached between us."

And Lady Agatha walked off leaving Magnus to think over what had passed, his mother's anger, and his inability to do anything about it.

Magnus's mind was a little ruffled for a moment, but the prospect of the trip with Alessandro had a soothing effect on him until, completely restored to his former feelings, he could not think about it with anything but with unalloyed joy.

CHAPTER XII

Magnus and Alessandro set off the next morning in pursuit of repose and joy at last. Joy in the present company was certain. It could overcome any mishap that may arise during the long journey. And along the way, an incident did occur which could have spoiled the trip if Alessandro had not been on hand. On the motorway, Magnus became aware that people were gesturing as they overtook him, pointing at the van. At first, he ignored it; Gwendolen was often noticed by motorists for her age, her looks, and her slow pace. But then it dawned on him that the gesturing may be pointing out something serious, and so they pulled up at the next service station to find out that the exhaust tail pipe had fallen off and was trailing behind them. Alessandro, much to Magnus's relief, lay down at the back of the van straightaway, pushed the tail pipe back into position, and tightened the screws that held the clamps together.

The latter part of the journey revealed the charming views of Derbyshire, its eminences, its deep dales, its winding rivers, its green escarpments on which sheep gambolled. Alessandro was in admiration of the scenery, all so different from his parched native Sicily, so much wetness, so much water, and those dear little black-headed sheep. Everything was approved of, and Magnus felt satisfied he was taking his friend to a lovely place.

They saw all the wonders of the county, Matlock Bath and the cable cars dangling from the Heights of Abraham, a veritable little Switzerland. In Matlock, they sauntered into bric-a-brac shops where Alessandro bought a pretty wood-turned lamp which he said would always remind him of this trip. Magnus found the Spode Chinese rose teapot he'd be looking for to complete his tea set.

The shopping was a success and so they wended their way to the town of Bakewell where Magnus had spent many happy family holidays. There, they had a lunch of delicious Austrian cheesy sausages in a bun and the most delicious apple strudel this side of the Channel. The owners of the "Tiroler Stuberl"—for that was what it was called—remembered Magnus from when he was a teenage boy and made much of him. It was lovely to have him back here and please make sure you say goodbye before you leave. There was now no room for a Bakewell pudding, that upside-down cake the result of an error, but they'd be back and make no mistake about it.

They drove to a nearby campsite perched high on the side of a hill which overlooked the Monsall Head viaduct and they spent the rest of the afternoon delighting in the views, resting from the journey and preparing for the night. The other campers and their assorted children made for jolly company in the campsite café where they had another bite to eat before going to bed. As the night fell on the camp, all became hushed. A cold spring night it would be in the hills and retreating into Gwendolen with a warm cup of cocoa to the flickering of candlelight was the epitome of comfort and cosiness.

As Magnus had talked excitedly about the plague village of Eyam—it is not the object of this work to give an account of what happened there—it was planned that they should visit the next day and go on a walk on Eyam Moor which included the Barrel Inn pub. To Eyam, therefore, they would go the next day.

Magnus, as they drove along, watched for the first appearance of the village. The High Street seemed not have changed since he'd last visited with his family, the same rows of honey-coloured plague cottages, the same wooden stocks in the middle of the village. He remembered how his brother Aled had kindly submitted to playing the part of miscreant, inserting both his feet in the stocks. Magnus had sentenced Aled to one day's misery in the stocks for stealing apples from the nearby greengrocer. Passersby had gathered thinking it was a theatrical performance and one of them even offered Magnus some money which he'd been too embarrassed to accept.

They parked the camper van and climbed up the steep road towards Eyam Moor. The views from the Barrel Inn pub extended over the valley right up to the majestic wooded hills of Dark Peak near Buxton. As it was too early for lunch, they decided to go on a circular walk on the moor behind the pub. They would descend toward Grindleford, then ascend again towards the inn.

The path went through peaty, waterlogged terrain, and Magnus advised Alessandro to watch his step, or he might fall into a bog. What was a bog? As Magnus started going into explanations, his attention was suddenly drawn to a cow with her calf a few feet away, slowly ambling towards them.

As the path was too narrow for them to walk past the animals without spooking them, Magnus thought it prudent to take the lower path on the left which in any case seemed conveniently to rejoin the path they were on. As predicted, they soon found themselves back on the original path, having successfully avoided a direct confrontation with a cow that may have been protective of her calf.

They turned round expecting the pair to be plodding off undisturbed in the distance. Much to their surprise, cow and calf had made an about-turn and were now following them. Magnus and Alessandro quickened their pace whilst attempting not to run, but the cow likewise quickened hers, soon threatening to catch up with them. There was nothing for it. Magnus knew instinctively the cow was about to charge and pointed without speaking to a lower field where they could safely get over a fence. They ran to the barbed wire fence, the cow still making good progress and nearly catching up with them. Magnus used a stone as a foothold and cleared the fence. Alessandro jumped over the barbed wire, but his left leg sank in the soft, boggy mound of earth with his trousers entangled in the wire at the crotch. The cow by now had nearly reached him. Magnus screamed at the animal which puzzled her and slowed her progress. He grabbed his friend's trousers at the crotch, lowered the barbed wire, and disentangled him. Alessandro, thus freed, tumbled down on the other side and they both fell on the ground in a heap, Alessandro on top of Magnus. By that time the cow had lost interest, walking away with her calf, unperturbed.

Alessandro and Magnus remained on top of each other for what must have been half a minute, dazed, Magnus gazing at the wide expanse of blue sky, trying to avoid looking into Alessandro's eyes. A strange sequence of high-pitched metallic notes was coming down out of the sky. He squinted and in the light he could see the rustling of a small bird, a lark probably, against the pale, sun-engorged sky. A stream was bubbling away next to them. Alessandro, full of the grace of God that comes from relief at having a narrow escape, looked down at his friend.

"It's like we've landed in paradise. What a marvellous little valley."

Magnus leaned backward to stroke the droopy heads of white comfrey and in the next moment was lying full length next to Alessandro in the long, cool, dewy grass. The light was dazzling and forming bleached patches of grass all around him. If this was paradise, it was painful as well. His body seemed to be as on a rack, extended to transparency as if to let the eternal white light in.

"This place is otherworldly. Are we alive? Is this real?" Magnus said.

"Magnus, are you feeling all right?"

"All manner of things will be well, Alessandro. This is a place of enchantment and this is where we will always live."

Alessandro looked at his friend and he, too, was filled with a sense of complete goodness, a sense of being held, like a nut, in the palm of a hand. Magnus slowly placed his hand on his friend's knee.

"Alessandro, do you want me to make love to you? I want to."

"You may regret it."

"Please let me. I know you want to."

"You said you loved me spiritually."

"But how can you bear such an innocent love?"

"Do you remember when you read 'Ode on a Grecian Urn' to me and you said you'd rather not win your goal so that you may love forever and love may never fade away? I feel a bit like that, frozen in time, yet knowing I can never love another."

As he looked at the burbling stream and heard the lark's metallic song up above, it came to Magnus: there were two possibilities. They could cultivate their spiritual friendship, as St. Aelred of Rievaulx called it, or he could become Alessandro's lover. There were not two possibilities. There were three. He could continue to have this public life with Alessandro as just a friend. Magnus began to have this little idea, somewhere lodged in his mind, that he would soon know clearly which of these choices was the right one.

At that moment, his phone vibrated on silent in his trouser pocket. It was a text message from his mother. Aled had been rushed to hospital after what seemed an epileptic fit. A brain tumour was suspected which, if confirmed by a scan, would be operated on either tomorrow or the next day. There was no time to lose. Can they please return to Norfolk? Another text. Magnus read as follows:

"'I'm afraid I have bad news for you. It's now been confirmed that Aled has a brain tumour. He will be operated on tomorrow in the afternoon. Although his headache has now subsided, the prognosis is not good. Even if the tumour turns out to be benign, Aled may be cognitively impaired. We are all so terribly upset here. I do hope you will return soon, though I dare not hope it will be before Aled's operation. Do get back to me.'"

They walked back down to the village in shocked silence, climbed up into Gwendolen, and left Derbyshire as if it had all been a dream, a revel sadly ended. Alessandro offered to drive as Magnus was in no fit state to do so and Magnus, relieved, felt once again in the hands of his beloved friend. This gave him time to reply to his mother. They were on their way and would be in Norfolk late this evening in time to see Aled before the operation. During the whole of the journey, Magnus's thoughts and prayers were never far away from his brother. Fixed in his anguished mind, they made any interlude of comfort impossible. Alessandro's expert driving meant that they soon reached Holton Hall where Lady Agatha was surprised to see them back so soon.

CHAPTER XIII

Magnus jumped out of Gwendolen and embraced his mother. Not a moment was lost in asking about Aled. Magnus's eyes filled with tears as Lady Agatha recounted what had happened. There was no further news. Isabella had been at the hospital since yesterday and ought to be relieved.

"Where are the children?" asked Magnus.

"Upstairs. They've been very good. They'll be pleased to see you."

"Are they aware of how serious the situation is?"

"Tristan is, of course, Owain less so. They've eaten and ought to be in bed soon, especially Owain."

"I'll get him ready for bed. You look worn out. You should go to bed, too."

Lady Agatha, however, assured him that she was very well especially now that he was here. She'd be able to drive to Norwich before dark. Come to think of it, the darkness did not bother her, her eyesight being the one thing that never failed her.

"Do be careful, Mother."

"I will, not to worry."

In the kitchen they were soon joined by Alessandro who had parked Gwendolen and unloaded a few bags.

"Alessandro has been most expeditious in his driving. It's thanks to him that we're here so early. I was in no fit state to drive," said Magnus.

"Thank you, Alessandro," said Lady Agatha warmly. "This was really most kind of you."

"Not at all, it was the least I could do. Any news of Aled?"

"I'm afraid not. I'm going to the Norfolk and Norwich now. Isabella has been there since yesterday and needs to be relieved."

"Do you want me to drive you to Norwich?"

"No, that won't be necessary. You stay with Magnus. You need a rest, too, after all the driving. In any case, I would not want to be stuck there without my car."

And with these words, Lady Agatha left the room and set off for the hospital to see her son.

When she was gone, Alessandro put his arm round Magnus's shoulders.

"Shall we attend to the children?" he asked.

"You go first, you're good with them."

As Alessandro entered the nursery, Magnus could hear the children's cries of joyful surprise. He joined them later and more screams ensued as well as various capers and other demonstrations of jollity. This earnest welcome warmed his heart and he looked at Alessandro. "Uncle A" as they called him was still being feted and before going to bed the children were regaled with the story of the charging cow in which Magnus figured as the hero of the day saving Uncle A from undoubted goring.

After Owain went to bed, which took all of Uncle A's firmness and persuasion, Tristan asked for more news of his father. At fourteen, he understood the gravity of the situation and was consequently more subdued than his brother. Alessandro uttered words of comfort which reassured him that there was still hope, that the tumour may be benign, and that there was still a chance Aled may pull through unscathed. Magnus seeing Alessandro's behaviour with Tristan had yet one more proof of his gentleness and his steadiness of purpose. He got both children to bed; there were no cries, no remonstrations. All happened swiftly and calmly, simply because the children knew Alessandro had resolved that it should.

Magnus, having received such a lesson on how to deal with his nephews, expressed his desire to go and pray in Holton Hall Church. It was agreed that Alessandro would stay in the hall until

Magnus's return. In any case, they'd probably both end up staying overnight as it was unlikely Lady Agatha would return this evening.

Magnus set off immediately. There was no need for a torch. In the moonlit night, the gravelled path seemed like a white ribbon of light that led right up the hillock to the church. He'd walked this way so many times since he was a boy that all seemed familiar down to the very potholes under his feet. Something like a categorical imperative compelled him to go to church now. Presently, he went into the half-ruined building, and sat down in one of the pews. He stared at the wooden rood screen in the obscurity of the church. The medieval paintings, bleached by time, cast a ghostly light all around. As his eyes became used to the darkness, Magnus could see the golden reredos with the painting that had always fascinated him ever since he'd first seen it as a child.

The painting depicted the Angels of Mons telling soldiers not to fear, that they would be protected in their retreat from the enemy. The painting now seemed gloriously luminous, the soldiers kneeling and fearfully listening to the Angels. Magnus knelt down, too. He felt the inevitability of his mortality as he'd never felt it before, the very finitude of his being. He felt, too, the very infinitude of his being, the love of God that surpasses all other loves. It was not so much a question of surpassing as of a sense that God's love, present in all earthly loves, made them possible, reflected them, refined them, intensified them. And he felt the need to examine himself. Had he been self-righteous at the university and closed the door on the possibility of reconciliation and forgiveness? Where there had been a desire for retribution, even for vengeance, there now seemed to be only a desert of moral blankness. If it weren't for God, Alessandro, Aled, and his family, he would turn himself silently into a monastery. And did he turn to God because there was no one to whom he could speak of all that gnawed at his contrite heart?

And he prayed intensely to be able to forgive so that he may be forgiven his own faults, his faults of superiority, of pride, of arrogance. He prayed the promise to become the servant of God, he prayed that Aled may pull through, and the two became inextricably linked: Alex's health and his own ordained ministry. It was not a deal, a mean bargain struck with an impassive God one tries to placate when in despair, the very God one ignores when all is well, the very God who wakes us up with his clarion call of pain. How wrong was it to ask for Aled's recovery in exchange of which he'd give his life to God? He wrestled with these ideas and knew then that his ordination would be an inevitable outcome, an event from which he could not subtract himself, a conduct which, if not performed to its rightful outcome, would be inexcusable.

He sat in St. Nicholas Church crying for Aled as he had not cried for anyone before. And just then the possibility of Aled's death seemed more awful than his own. He could not die, or live impaired forevermore. In the hours following his mother's text message, Magnus had thought he would go mad. He'd been so deliriously happy lying next to Alessandro. Was he being punished for this love?

As Alessandro drove in silence, Magnus had resolved not to tell him of his misgivings. This hung round his neck like an albatross. There should be no guilt. He could see this now. And he should share this with Alessandro. He could not bear it alone and this too would be resolved by his decision to become a priest. There should be no guilt. There should be freedom from the law. He was forgiven and he should tell Alessandro. He must tell Alessandro everything, or else he would know something was wrong.

He got up to leave the church, sorrowful yet joyful. All would be well. He walked up the aisle towards the door. A plaque in honour of an old Norfolk family asked him to pray for their souls. He sat down again and prayed. This was God's call, his call, in a world of brokenness, to a life of ceaseless prayer for all.

Magnus walked back to the hall. The drawing room was lit up and Olive, the golden retriever, was warming herself by the dying embers of the hearth. When she saw Magnus, she turned on her back wanting to be stroked. Although she was Lady Agatha's dog, she'd always had divided loyalties and spent many a night with Magnus at the rectory. Sensing something was extraordinary this night, she went into the kitchen and picked up the soft cushion on which she usually slept. She climbed up the stairs with it in her mouth, and Magnus followed her in silence. The dog led him to a dimly lit room next to the children's bedrooms. Alessandro was already fast asleep in one of the beds. Another bed had been made hastily for Magnus to sleep in. The dog dropped her cushion between the two beds and curled round on it. This is where she would sleep. Magnus climbed into bed next to her, gave her one more gentle stroke of his hand. He crossed himself as he lay down and fell to praying again. Sleep overcame him before he could say "Amen."

CHAPTER XIV

The drive to the hospital was to happen very early in the morning. Isabella had returned during the night and when she met Magnus and Alessandro at breakfast, Aled's health was talked of as sadly deteriorating. The operation was scheduled after lunch and Magnus must lose no time in setting off.

"I'll drive you to the hospital, if you want," said Alessandro. "I can drop you off outside and use the free car park near the university."

The novelty of being driven to Norwich by his friend and the prospect of seeing Aled had its uplifting effect on Magnus's spirits, were it not for the fact that he had agreed to meet with Dr. Sedley afterwards. Magnus had decided to hand in his resignation letter. To find himself compelled to account for his decision to leave in the presence of a man he so intensely disliked was mortifying. Yet, the thought of his future in holy orders allowed him to proceed with the journey with more equanimity.

There was no end of pleasant chat between him and Alessandro as they drove through the undulating countryside of North Norfolk where the eye cannot rove without seeing a church in which God's love has been known and faith has been lived for thousands of years. The chat turned to ordination training, of course, and Alessandro held his friend's hand whilst holding the wheel with the other.

They soon arrived at the Norfolk and Norwich Hospital. Magnus was directed to Aled's room in the neurology department; his case had been judged so severe that a bed in a ward had been ruled out. Very exceptionally, an eminent visiting surgeon from Cambridge had offered to conduct the operation, and Aled would not have to be transferred to the hospital there. Exceptionally too, Lady Agatha had been allowed to stay overnight by her son's side before the operation, and she was brimming over with gratitude.

Although Magnus had been told about Aled's deteriorating state, nothing prepared him for the shock of seeing his altered appearance. He sat in bed hunched forward, not making eye contact with anyone. When he realised Magnus had arrived, he cheered up a little, lifting his head occasionally to meet his brother's eyes. His hair had already been shaved, and he looked monastically pensive and sad. Magnus touched his arm lightly.

"All will be well, you can be sure of that," he said in a barely audible whisper.

"I know, now you're here."

Aled's depressed spirits seemed instantly calmed, and Lady Agatha, who had only sat quietly by the bed not knowing what to say, was also comforted: Magnus, the preferred companion in sickness.

"I have something to say to you," said Aled.

"Please, Aled, do not exert yourself."

"No, no, this is very important, if I should die . . ."

"But you won't."

"No, wait, you must hear me out. It is my wish that the estate be looked after by you and Alessandro. Mother will tell you the rest."

"It's fine, Aled, of course we will do as you wish, but now please rest, and don't worry about anything."

As he said this, Aled gave a wan smile and his head sank back once more into his chest. Magnus took his hand gently and kneeling by the bed pressed it against his face. He looked up at Aled, and saw that he was still smiling, accepting of his brother's comforting touch.

A nurse came in and administered a sedative. As somnolence took over, Lady Agatha, who had remained silent throughout, rose from her chair and kissed her son on his forehead; Aled was wheeled out of the room.

Magnus brought his chair nearer to his mother's and they sat holding hands in the anguished silence that words cannot break. The pain of having perhaps lost a son, a beloved brother, imposed itself so utterly on their consciousness that it made any other form of communication between them impossible.

A nurse came in to tell them that the operation had started and that all was fine. Aled would be taken to intensive care afterwards. It would be better to visit the next day when he'd be brought back to his room. In the meantime, the hospital would keep them informed of any development.

As they prepared to leave, Alessandro walked in.

"I'm afraid the car is parked miles away," he said apologetically.

"Sorry you missed him, Alessandro. He just been taken into the operating theatre," said Lady Agatha.

"Oh, but I did get to see him in the corridor. He waved at me though he seemed out of it already and I waved back."

It was agreed that Alessandro would accompany Lady Agatha to Holton Hall in her own car, and Magnus would drive back in Gwendolen after seeing Dr. Sedley.

"Will you be all right?" inquired Alessandro.

"I'll be fine. I'm feeling quite equal to the task actually," said Magnus. "I'm looking forward to it in some curious sort of way. I shouldn't gloat really, but I have a feeling that Dr. Sedley will be discomfited."

"Now, before you leave, Mag," said Lady Agatha, "there's one more thing I need to say to you both. Aled's arrangements about Holton Hall are, of course, totally in accordance with what normally happens in such circumstances. But I know that what he really wanted to say was that you should not have anything to do with Henrietta. He just simply could not get round to saying it. I suppose he thought he may be imposing on you, or assuming too much. In any case, here's a text message I received from her a few hours before you arrived which I think you should read."

Lady Agatha handed her phone to Magnus. The text read:

"Hi, just heard the ghastly news about Aled and thought I'd find out how he's doing. I was utterly shocked to hear of an irreversible decline from Rev. Bold. One silver lining, I suppose, is that Holton Hall is in good hands with Magnus. Do let him know that I'd almost be able to forgive his becoming a vicar, were he to take over as head of Holton Hall. Status and importance could not fall into safer hands . . ."

The rest was valedictory, and equally free and inappropriate. Magnus could not read any further, so disgusted was he by the tenor of the message.

Lady Agatha said, "I have replied to the effect that Aled was doing well and that we're praying for a complete recovery. In the meantime, you and Alessandro would be in charge of Holton Hall, and she should wait for your instructions to come within the next few days."

"Did Aled know about this message?"

"He did, but didn't have the strength to enter into details."

"We cannot have such an interested person who thinks nothing of importance but money and position as our accountant."

"This is what Aled thinks, but could not bring himself to express explicitly. He'd long suspected Henrietta of being mercenary in her attentions to him. She would not have balked at destroying his marriage to Isabella incidentally, if she'd had the opportunity."

"I had a presentiment of this at that fateful picnic."

"You've been altogether far more intuitive about this than I have, I must say, and I hope you're not too cross with me for being so sanguine about her."

"Of course not," said Magnus, pressing his mother to his heart, "but we can only give thanks for Aled's constancy. There would have been no end of the evil let loose upon our family if he had in any way been swayed by her wiles."

"My dear Magnus, my dear Alessandro, now I shall be comfortable," said Lady Agatha.

Magnus looked fondly at his mother and his friend as they walked away arm in arm to Lady Agatha's car. There was something of Jesus's favourite disciple about it, the beloved John.

As he himself walked through the covered pathways of Paine Anglia campus, he felt the weight of his own cross lift off his shoulders, the weight of his mother's erstwhile disapproval, her incessant call to marriage now supplanted by Alessandro and his disinterested friendship.

CHAPTER XV

Now displayed on somewhat lurid signs was the new name for the School of "Communication Studies, Translation, and Intercultural Communication." The acronym "CSTIC" had indeed stuck, and as Magnus approached his department remembering all the pointless arguments, his heart sank a little, and he became melancholy; it must be said that the change from "Linguistics" had made little difference to student recruitment. He entered the corridor and saw Daphne who, as was customary, had left her office door open. This lifted his spirits. It had been almost a month's break and he was expected with much impatience. He had scarcely walked past her office when she fell upon him in a big affectionate hug.

"My dear Magnus, now I shall he happy again! We've got so much to catch up on!"

"It's lovely to see you, too, Daphne, but I'm meeting with Dr. Sedley in a few minutes, so if there's anything I should know . . ."

This was invitation enough for Daphne. She was by no means a systematic, or particularly coherent, narrator, but Magnus was able to understand as much of the circumstances as he needed for his meeting with Sedley. It transpired that Professor Lehideux had refused point-blank to give her and Magnus a formal apology for inciting other colleagues against them. Daphne had given the go-ahead for legal action to be taken, but in the end, Lehideux had accepted the university's generous package of early retirement and left. The last time she'd seen him he'd ripped up all the "egalitarian" name labels out of the pigeonholes, and stood surrounded by what looked like snowflakes on the floor, mumbling to himself distractedly in French. There was more to be said about his departure, but Daphne did not have time to elaborate on it and it was too odious to mention anyway.

Professor Lehideux's state of mind Magnus could hardly imagine and, albeit repelled by what he was hearing, he couldn't help feeling for him; such misery, leading to what may be a dishonourable end.

Another moment and Magnus was outside Dr. Sedley's office who met him with looks of genuine kindness. He was an altogether altered man. He had lost a great deal of weight, having been ill during his sabbatical. Nearly lost his eyesight and been diagnosed with dangerous high levels of sugar in his blood. But he was better now, on a strict diet of wholesome sugar-free food and gentle exercise.

"'Gentle exercise' is the operative word, mind, because of my failing heart," he said, "but it's put things in perspective, you know. I am relieved this nasty business with Professor Lehideux is resolved now. You see, with him it was like a war he was determined you should lose, a fight for atheism and republicanism, I think that's how he thought of it."

Magnus remembered the egalitarian pigeonholes and smiled.

"Well, all I can say is that I was never that involved in much of it, really. You've gained by it, mind, being permanent and all that, but you'll be stepping in dead man's shoes, in a manner of speaking—that is, we'd like you to teach Lehideux's translation class next semester."

"Ah! But I shan't."

Dr. Sedley put on his pained, disappointed look. Surely now that his post was made permanent, Magnus could not refuse to help in what were after all exceptional circumstances.

"I mean, I will not be able to take Lehideux's class because I shan't be at Paine Anglia. I came to see you to hand in my resignation as of today. My brother Aled has fallen ill, and is being operated on as we speak. I shall be needed to manage the estate for a while."

The look of affected disappointment changed into one of stunned silence. Nothing more was said except for the usual and anticipated expressions of commiseration.

Magnus walked back from Dr. Sedley's office, relieved and reflecting that here was a man who, albeit not completely reformed, seemed to have begun the process of examining himself; a vitiated mind no doubt, but one that as a result of pain and disease looked like it was on the mend. Maybe the future with him as a colleague would have been a pleasure, and this was something possibly to regret. But what an acquaintance with the three of them it had been: all, despite Dr. Sedley's disavowals, guilty of fomenting. What a desperate triumvirate! And yet, when he thought of them as individuals, each one of them could be divorced from the sin of ambition that had united them. Once they must have nurtured ideals of academic excellence, once they must even have had their students' interest at heart.

And so he went back to his office and collected as many books as he could carry in an attempt to begin clearing it out before his departure. He said a perfunctory goodbye to Daphne and promised to arrange to meet her again soon.

"Our MA in second language learning is starting next autumn and we were rather hoping you may be delivering a course on 'Language and Literature,'" said Daphne.

"Daphne, I shan't be here next autumn. I've just handed in my resignation to Dr. Sedley. My brother Aled has fallen ill and I am needed at Holton Hall."

There was a little scream and much protestation, but in the end it all seemed the right thing to do. Magnus may be able to contribute unofficially, maybe some tutoring.

As he left campus, he thought of the many times he had done so as a form of deliverance from the shackles of a prison. This time, when he would not return, was fast approaching. The cycle of arrivals and departures that punctuates our lives rarely yields a sense of relief. To resign from his research post just as it was being made permanent for something as formless as ordination training was beginning to feel unwise. Most of the people he knew would think it was a foolish thing to do. But as these wavering thoughts assailed him, the memory of his miraculous night in Holton Hall Church came back to him. He had to leave. There was no other way. There was a model for leaving; he must rejoice like Jesus's disciples.

And so it is true that Magnus, as he left Paine Anglia University, books in one hand, his old leather satchel in another, suffered from regret and grief over what might have been. But there was great comfort in knowing that a higher authority would not relent in seeking him out. This was not a plunge into the unknown. Here was his own Pentecost.

There was the conviction, too, that it would take many years before Paine Anglia regained the harmony it once had. It had become a community of irreconcilable rights. And those who articulated them the most vociferously usually won. There were times like this before, inquisitorial times when individuals prowled around seeking whom they may devour; these were the worst of times.

On his return to Holton Hall, Magnus had one last important call to make. This was to Rev. Dr. Leigh. The reverend doctor was an affable man who, having done much good in the Holton Benefice, had nonetheless failed to impress the hierarchy. Maybe it was his live-and-let-live approach which jarred. If the truth be known, he felt a little weighed down by recent developments in the Church of England. He had a particular distaste for moral busybodies, and over the years, had come to the conclusion, like his favourite Mr. Lewis, that the most intolerable of tyrannies must be the one sincerely exercised for the good of its victims.

Magnus had a deep font of respect for this churchman who, though he may remain obscure and leave no mark on history, would have altered the lives of many parishioners, including his own. And as he was about to knock on his front door, he was reminded of an observation at the close of *Middlemarch* that the good of the world depends on "unhistoric acts" for which we must be thankful because we owe our comforts largely to those who "lived faithfully a hidden life, and rest in unvisited tombs."

On opening the door, Rev. Leigh's face brightened into a smile from ear to ear.

"I must say I was expecting you," he said.

"You were?"

"I hope I'm not presuming too much in thinking you may be here in connection with ordination training."

"I suppose you've heard it from my mother."

"And from others, too. I thought of talking to you about it many times, but in cases like this, it's better if you make the first step, don't you think?"

"You make it sound like a marriage proposal."

"Ah, yes, yes, and you may get turned down. Always be prepared for that. But I would be delighted if you would allow me to get the ball rolling. Discernment can take up to a year, sometimes even longer."

"That's rather drawn out."

"But necessary. Your call will take shape in the hands of God, one way or another, and what you're undertaking now will change in the course of discernment. May I ask you a few questions? You see, these are questions that you will inevitably be asked during your interviews with different representatives of the Church and it is just as well to be prepared for them."

"Please, go ahead."

"One of the questions concerns marriage. At your age, people are mostly either married or divorced and as you are neither, you may be asked why you have not married."

"I have not found the right person," Magnus blurted out, reddening and thinking of Alessandro.

"Ah, well, yes, but there is the question of Alessandro. May I ask if you are in a gay relationship?"

"No."

"Good. Good. As you know, the Church has been tearing itself apart over these issues. There are those who advocate gay marriage, those who can only go as far as a blessing, and those who vehemently oppose all of it. Are you aware of the current position of our Church as far as sexual morality is concerned?"

"Yes, and my relationship with Alessandro conforms to it in that we are celibate and not married. I tend to think of marriage as pleasing to God in the context of procreation, but celibacy may, as St. Paul advises, be a higher good for non-married people."

"Quite, quite," replied Dr. Leigh, "but I suppose you needn't go into *that* amount of detail; just say that you are fully aware of the Church's stance on sexual morality, and that you intend to abide by it. You may want to add that you are not called to marriage, but to building a sense of community amongst your parishioners. That should do it, for the time being at least."

"Sorry, I just got carried away."

"Not at all, not at all, I do want you to get through the selection process which, although it is ultimately in the hands of God, can be full of pitfalls nowadays . . . Yes, yes, well, once you've been accepted for ordination training, God is your authority. You see, it's always been a question of who has authority in the church, the pope, the archbishop, the king. Even Jesus was asked. But, of course, as he was the authority, he didn't need to 'have' it, if you see what I mean."

Magnus wasn't sure he quite saw what he meant, though the distinction must be one between "having" and "being." Clearly, the reverend doctor was enjoying this.

"Now, where are you on obedience? Not a fashionable word, I believe."

"I am always happy to obey my superiors; it relieves me of responsibility for my own deeds."

"Yes, yes, but you must not be slavishly obedient, though my advice in these matters may not be the best way to becoming a bishop."

"I am not aspiring to that."

"Hehehe . . . just as well, the career progression is a rather steep pyramid: many priests, very few bishops, and two archbishops in England. Not much fun for your career priest. By the way, talking about careers, Rev. Bold has been made a chaplain in one of the Cambridge Colleges, Peterhouse, I think."

"He should thrive there."

"You're a Cambridge man and, of course, you'll know about these things."

Magnus smiled at the thought of Rev. Bold in a college known for its same-sex antics.

"Well, I think we've covered all the necessary ground," said the reverend doctor. "I hope you don't think you've gone from the frying pan into the fire. Academia is currently beset with many problems, but the Church of England isn't far behind. I fear the days of the 'Humpty Dumpty' school of language are upon us when words mean just what the Church of England chooses them to mean. Alice, of course, was right to observe that it is unlikely you can make words mean so many different things . . . Oh, well, let us pray."

Magnus bowed his head, crossed himself, and received the blessing he'd so enjoyed hearing in his Cambridge College:

"Lord, as Magnus embarks on his journey of discernment, may you bless him and make your face to shine upon him and be gracious unto him; may you look down with favour on his calling, and the blessing of God Almighty, Father, Son, and Holy Spirit. Amen."

A feeling of warmth suffused Magnus as the blessing was uttered; there was not any doubt; it was simply right to do what he was doing. The words in the mouths of priests may waywardly be losing their holy origins, but all would be well nonetheless. Of this he was assured.

CHAPTER XVI

And so this story has come to an end. It is an end suited to the gently rolling hills of Norfolk, not the precipitous valleys of the North, nor the tempestuous shores of the West. Everybody in it, neither wholly bad nor wholly good, will be restored to some form of happiness, even if not the one they had had in mind.

My Magnus at this time, I know, must have been a very happy man. He returned to Holton Hall for good, loved by all around him and useful in the running of the estate which followed Aled's operation. The main source of his delight was Alessandro who continued in everybody's approbation including that of Lady Agatha. In the early years, he occasionally had to go back to Sicily to look after his ageing mother. At his own University of Catania he became widely recognised as the authority in the field of cryptology and his academic career flourished. Magnus joined him in conferences whenever he could and relished the vivid colours of the Mediterranean, the fierceness of Mount Etna, and the coolness of "granita" sorbets.

But Magnus and Alessandro often experienced the cultural shocks that came from a lack of order and much corruption on European soil. The rural, disciplined, and harmonious world of Holton Hall beckoned then, and they were always relieved to return to it.

Another great comfort was Aled's health which he gradually regained without any loss of his faculties. In time he would take back control of the estate. Nothing, however, could surpass Magnus's joy when he found out that he had been accepted for ordination training. On hearing the news, he sank to his knees thanking God. In a few months, he would be bound for theological college in Cambridge where he would start on the second year of the Tripos in Theology.

These were circumstances which reconciled Lady Agatha to herself, assuaging her sense of what was lost. A parent and conscious of the limitations of her judgement concerning marriage, she was the one who had found it hardest to accept the new arrangements. She felt she ought to have been more alert to Henrietta's scheming and that her son's feelings had been made sufficiently clear to her to render her guilty of wrongly encouraging the relationship between them. With these reflections and intimations of her own mortality, she, however, took no time in finding great comfort in Alessandro who became increasingly useful to her as her adviser and companion. In Alessandro's usefulness, in Magnus's excellence, and in Aled's and Isabella's continued expert management of the estate, Lady Agatha had every good reason to rejoice in what had finally come to pass.

As for Henrietta, she opened a delicatessen near the coast in Wiveton on the way to Holkham which she called "The Picnic Basket." This became very successful with all the tourists getting a meal together before going to the beach. She sold homemade cakes, pies, expensive loaves of bread, and, ironically, Holton Hall's "Mrs. Church" unpasteurised cheese which had become so popular in the region that visitors kept asking for it. She started stocking it with much reluctance, and every time she sold it, was reminded of that disastrous picnic in Holkham Beach. She let it be known that she'd lived in Buckingham Palace and was connected to the queen to all who cared to hear. She'd had hopes to marry Magnus, and especially so if Aled did not recover, but had been so mercenary in the process as to ruin it all. She never quite found the elder brother in charge of an estate, though this wasn't for want of trying.

Rev. Bold's career as a chaplain in Peterhouse College ended abruptly. The allegations of a scandal were never quite substantiated, but nonetheless became the subject of momentous consultations and negotiations with the college. The Bishop of Ely thought it wiser to remove him from Cambridge altogether. It ended in Rev. Bold's resolving to quit ministry to devote himself to charity work in an international organisation. It is reasonable to suppose that he would fit in well, at least for a time, in a context where a lack of integrity and a propensity to ignore the wishes of elected governments are often valued. Rev. Bold's removal from Cambridge was a great comfort to Magnus. He was relieved that a man who had increasingly lost favour in his esteem would have no influence in a society where he would otherwise have been bound to meet him.

Magnus did go back to campus to see Daphne who had yet more tales with which to regale him.

Dr. Grieve, who still had not published anything, had been made "Head of Learning and Teaching"; Daphne could not figure how or why, but then the ways of Paine Anglia University were not her ways. Dr. Grieve had claimed Dr. Sedley's office was haunted, but shut up about it in the end as this was threatening to cost him his promotion with the highly secular university authorities.

Sheena Easton went back to Australia. She was running out of trees with which to offset her carbon emissions. Out of desperation, she'd even planted Leylandii at the back of her house, but they'd grown so fast and so tall as to overshadow her neighbours' garden and she'd had to have them felled at great expense to herself. Her safe space scheme at Paine Anglia had not worked out so well, either. In this she'd been a victim of her own success. So many "safe spaces" had sprouted up that they could not all be properly supervised, and some students were getting up to some decidedly unsafe practices in them. The university authorities had to close them down.

"There was quite a nasty side to her, too," said Daphne. "She raised a grievance against me with HR because she overheard me say that veganism was idiotic. Do you remember when we were chatting about Aled's delicious unpasteurised cheese?"

"You were getting done for that?"

"Absolutely, and there was talk of me having to be trained on how not to offend colleagues."

"Good God, PAU sounds more like the Stasi every day."

"Well, the whited sepulchres get undone in the end. 'Even 'butter-would-not-melt-in-my-mouth-100-percent-compliant' Hilda van der Linden is leaving under a cloud! Do you remember how she used to go on about working until late in the evening? Well, she most certainly did, with some of her male MA students, except . . . well, not in the way we thought. Word got round from the porters who'd watched her from their top floor office. Is 'peeping' the word?" Magnus confirmed it was, feeling queasy.

"But, there's worse," said Daphne, who by now was unstoppable. "She published her best MA students' dissertations as her own work. One of her students was accused of plagiarism and it was tracked all the way back to her."

Professor Lehideux's seedy, though not illegal, material found on his work computer will not be dwelt on: too odious a subject for these pages. He was regretted by no one at Paine Anglia, and his removal from the university became such a felicity that, had he not left in his wake unhappy memories of bullying, one could, as others have said before me, almost have approved of the evil which produced so much good. It ended with him choosing to remove himself and his wife to an exclusive and, most definitely not egalitarian, gated community in France. As others have said before me again, it may be reasonably surmised that being shut up together in such close proximity became their unending punishment.

Dr. Sedley continued to mend his ways and became a mentor and a favourite to all his younger colleagues, even disregarding opportunities for his own promotion. He is now luxuriating in his office, no longer a head of school, but actually reading in his field, eating sensibly, and doing good.

Finally, Daphne has received Dr. Coffey's many demonstrations of affection kindly and Magnus was delighted to hear that they would soon marry. And would he officiate or at least be there when it happened? Of course, he would.

With so much divine grace bestowed upon all and as much happiness as their limited exile on earth could afford, Holton Hall was home to true affection and comfort. On the death of Rev. Dr. Leigh, Magnus was appointed to the living of the very church where he had first received his call. There, he was priested and Alessandro, who had never been able to approach St. Nicholas without being reminded of Rev. Bold's unwelcome advances, grew to love it as anywhere else in Holton Hall. There too, Alessandro came to be accepted as Magnus's partner and friend. It must be said that there was more burning tenderness to be found in this marriage of likeness than in many more official contracts between men and women.

When Alessandro saw Magnus robed in his priestly vestments for the first time, he knew he had lost him to the Lord. But this awareness of eternity made their earthly relationship in the parsonage of Holton Hall more thoroughly perfect than it could possibly have been without it.

FINIS

www.ingramcontent.com/pod-product-compliance
Lightning Source LLC
LaVergne TN
LVHW020652100826
845148LV00012B/2441

* 9 7 9 8 3 8 5 2 7 0 9 6 5 *